The Over-the-Hill
WITCH

The Over-the-Hill WITCH

By Ruth Calif
Illustrated by Joan Holub

PELICAN PUBLISHING COMPANY
GRETNA 1990

Library of Congress Cataloging-in-Publication Data

Calif, Ruth.
    The over-the-hill witch / by Ruth Calif; illustrated by Joan Holub.
        p.   cm.
    Summary: Ten-year-old Gary moves to a small Ozark commu-
nity and becomes embroiled in rumors about old Mama Spoonaker,
who is accused of practicing witchcraft and casting spells of re-
venge.
    ISBN 0-88289-754-3
    [1. Witchcraft—Fiction.   2. Ozark Mountains—Fiction.]
I. Holub, Joan, ill.   II. Title.
PZ7.C12860vf   1990   89-35371
[Fic]—dc20   CIP
                                                            AC

Manufactured in the United States of America
Published by Pelican Publishing Company, Inc.
1101 Monroe Street, Gretna, Louisiana 70053

For my mother,
GERTRUDE LAMMERT,
who was always
there for me

CONTENTS

The Over-the-Hill
WITCH

CHAPTER ONE

SCHOOLHOUSE BLUES

GARY LEE BENSON shivered in the darkness as he tried to see around him from the bale of hay on which he sat. He wasn't usually afraid of the dark, but it sure was scary out here! He clutched his dog closer beside him. Spike whined, then gave his master a lick on the cheek.

"Can't see nothing," Gary muttered.

He had talked his mother into letting him camp out for the night in the shed that housed their milk cow and a supply of baled hay, but he hadn't remembered just how spooky night could become. Outside, some little animal squealed his anguish as a predator took his life, and a shiver ran down Gary's back. An owl hooted in the distance and Gary scrunched farther down, pulling his dog to lie beside him.

"Stay put, Spike," he said into the silken ear.

"Spike" was short for "Benson's Beachboy Baron," the registered name of the black and white springer spaniel who was Gary's constant companion except

1

when Gary was in school. Spike usually waited on the front porch for the school bus to bring his master home.

Then Gary shook his head and straightened his back. After all, he was ten years old and almost a man. There was nothing for him to fear, was there?

"Sit up, Spike," he said sternly. "Mustn't slump."

Suddenly, shining yellow eyes appeared above him and seemed to bore into his wide-eyed stare. Spike growled. With a yelp, Gary slid down from the hay and hightailed it to the house. Spike looked uncertainly from the glowing eyes to his departing master, then leaped to the ground and ran after Gary.

It was fortunate for both boy and dog that the door had been left unlatched, for Gary would not have waited for his mother to answer a summons. He had to get inside! Spike scooted in under Gary's feet so he wouldn't get caught in the closing door. Experience had taught him it was painful.

The light came on and Gary's mother stood inside the kitchen looking at them. "What is it, honey?" she asked. "Have you decided not to camp out tonight?"

"I saw eyes!" he gasped.

"Eyes? What sort of eyes?"

"Big yellow ones!"

His mother smiled as she came to help him remove the coat he had bundled around him. "It was probably just a cat," she said soothingly, "but I'm glad you came in. I get a little afraid when I'm in here alone."

Gary's father had died six months before. He had left his wife and son a farm and a mortgage, but without him to care for it, Gary's mother decided it was best to sell the farm, pay off the mortgage, and move to the small town of Bellarosa. It would be best for Gary to go to school and for her to sew for the townswomen who could not do their own sewing.

Bellarosa was typical of the small settlements nestled in the Ozark Mountains. It was founded in the 1880s and lay in a valley ringed with the beautiful little mountains that changed colors with the seasons. The only industries were the stores that serviced surrounding farmers who came in for supplies every Saturday. During the week, only noises from the schoolyard broke the peace and quiet for the inhabitants—that and an occasional truck that lumbered in looking for the diesel station that had a sign on the freeway half a mile away.

"Would you like a glass of milk and some cookies?" Gary's mother asked. "Might help you to sleep better."

"Can Spike have some too?"

"Of course." She poured the glass full of milk, then a small bowl that she placed on the floor. Next came the cookie jar that she set on the table.

"Help yourself, honey, and give Spike a cookie if he wants one."

"Thanks, Mom." Gary grinned sheepishly as he remembered how he had nagged to sleep in the shed before his mother gave him permission. If the eyes he had seen belonged to a stray cat, he'd been a jerk to let them spook him. He swallowed the last of the cookie he had taken, gulped the last of his milk, then rose.

"Guess we'll sleep inside tonight, Mom. That old cat sure upset Spike."

His mother smiled a sort of sad smile and Gary knew she was thinking about his father. Bob Benson had been a happy man and a good farmer. Why did the old tractor have to suddenly rear up and dump him on the ground, then fall on top of him? He had been killed instantly. Just as quickly, Gary's mother seemed to forget how to laugh.

The Benson family had been a jolly bunch before the accident. Now there were smiles but no laughter, and Gary no longer felt like teasing his mother as he once had done. Now he had to figure out how to help her. He really missed his dad! How could he be the man of the house if old cat's eyes scared him in the dark? That was probably only a mouse that had squealed, although it had made a chill run down his back.

Gary picked up the bowl and put it and the glass into the sink. His mother waited until he and Spike had gone, then turned off the light and followed them up the stairs to the bedrooms, calling a soft good-night to Gary as he entered his room.

Gary looked around at the strangeness of his new room. The one on the farm had been cozy and small, but this one was large and horrid so far as he was concerned. The high ceiling and tall and narrow windows in the walls that made up the corner of the room looked weird. His bed that once had seemed so large now looked very small in the huge space.

Gary slowly undressed, then put on his pajamas before he went to stare out a window into the night. Few lights showed in the small town, but the ones that still remained lit were too close to suit him. On the farm he could look out his window and see only fields and trees and bright stars in the sky.

Tomorrow he would have to go to the school at the

other end of town and he dreaded facing new teachers and kids he didn't know. On the farm a bus had picked him up and carried him to the consolidated school in a larger town, but since they had moved to Bellarosa he would have to go to the town school. It had yet to be consolidated into a district school.

He sighed. His mother had said she would go with him on his first day to be sure he was signed in properly, but then he would be left on his own.

"Wish you could go to school with me, Spike," he muttered as he returned to his bed.

The dog had curled up at the foot of the bed but when Gary spoke, he wagged his tail and sat up. Good old Spike. He was always ready to do anything Gary wanted.

Slowly, Gary stretched out on his back and lay flat as he stared up at the ceiling. His eyes watered as he thought about his father. Why did he have to die? There were a lot of older people around. Why hadn't one of them died instead? The pale face of his father as he lay in the coffin came to mind and Gary wished he had never looked. He wanted to remember his dad as he looked while still alive—laughing, happy, loving his son and playing with him. Gary knuckled away the tears and rolled over onto his stomach. It was time to sleep. Spike whined and crawled up beside his master as though to comfort him.

The next morning Gary woke as a ray of sunshine poked itself through a window and into his face. He blinked, then realized where he was and sat up. Spike aped his action and Gary grinned.

"Time for you to go outside," he said, then led the way out of the room and down the stairs to the kitchen. There he opened the door and Spike ambled out into the yard. On his way back up the steps, Gary smiled at his mother coming down.

"Good morning, Gary," she said.

"Good morning, Mom."

"Better hurry. We're due at the school in an hour and I want you to eat a good breakfast."

"Okay, Mom. Will you let Spike in when he comes to the door? He'd better have breakfast, too."

"Sure. Wear some good clothes today so you'll make a good first impression."

"Oh, Mom!" Gary sighed, knowing she meant his suit. He would much rather wear his usual jeans and T-shirt. "None of the other kids will be wearing suits."

Mary Benson sighed, then said, "You're probably right. Wear your usual clothes, but put on clean ones."

"Okay, Mom."

Gary went happily on his way. He knew how kids treated strangers and one in a suit would have made matters worse. If he looked like them maybe they wouldn't be too unfriendly. It always took a while for a new kid to be accepted at any school, but he hoped he could make friends fast. Since his father's death, Gary had been too busy helping his mother to do much playing and he was lonely.

Inside his room he opened the closet and took out his high-tops, then went to the chest of drawers for a T-shirt and jeans and clean underwear. He stopped at the bathroom to comb his hair and brush his teeth, then went down the stairs to meet his mother.

After breakfast they walked the six blocks to the

school. Gary smiled at people who passed, but was answered with only stares of curiosity. In a town of this size, not many people moved into an old house.

The school was two-storied with tall narrow windows that shone in the morning sun. Inside, they walked into the principal's office and waited.

A tall gray-haired man walked over to them and asked, "May I help you, madam?"

Gary's mother smiled. "I hope so," she answered. "My son would like to attend your school. I am Mary Benson and this is Gary."

"How do you do, Mrs. Benson... Gary. I am John Dickens, principal of Bellarosa School." He shook both their hands and indicated they take seats beside his desk. "Now, if you have Gary's transcript from his last school, he can begin classes with us today."

"Of course," Mary said, opening her purse. "Here is the transfer and also his last report card."

A bell rang and through the open door Gary could see youngsters heading into school, then dividing into groups that went into classrooms and up the stairs to the second floor. He sighed, wishing he were back at his former school where he knew almost everybody. He liked school and he had an inquisitive mind that had to know the why and how and where of everything, but he also liked to have fun.

Mr. Dickens raised his eyebrows as he glanced at the card Mary Benson had given him, then looked at Gary. Now he rose and again shook her hand. "This is a very good report card, Mrs. Benson," he said with a smile. "I'm sure your son will fit in here very well."

After Gary's mother had gone, Mr. Dickens took Gary into one of the rooms and introduced him to his teacher, Miss Black, then handed her the papers he had brought.

She glanced at them and said, "My! Hello, Gary Benson." Then she turned to the class and introduced him to his classmates. "At recess you children can introduce yourselves to our new student, but for now, Gary, please sit here." She indicated an empty desk and he sat down.

"Now, children, please open your readers and continue with the chapter we began last week."

When she saw that all were occupied, she turned to Gary and said, "I'll go get you a set of books." She left and soon returned with the necessary textbooks.

"Thank you," Gary said, then reddened as he saw some of the other pupils turn to look at him.

"Turn to page 107, Gary. You just sit in with us today. You can look over the books this evening and catch up with where we are working."

"Yes'm." Gary saw that the books were the same as those he had at his last school, and he relaxed with a sigh of relief. At least he was familiar with the studies in his class. It was the unfamiliar things that worried him.

It seemed no time at all before a bell rang and the children rose and trooped out. Gary looked questioningly at the teacher.

"You may go, Gary," she said. "Get acquainted with your classmates."

Gary walked slowly from the room to the schoolyard. Now came the hard part. He approached a group of boys and smiled, hoping they would be friendly. "Hi, guys," he said.

The boys had broken off their talk at his approach

and now they stared at him. Gary shifted nervously, then one of the boys drew him into the circle.

"I'm Jimmy Allen," he said. "This is Billy Walker, John James, and Willie Haus."

Gary nodded at each in turn as he muttered "hi" to each name.

"Where you from?" Billy asked.

"A farm near Willoughby," Gary answered. "We just moved to town last week."

"What's your pa do?" Willie asked.

"He's dead."

There was a silence as the boys thought about this, then Jimmy said matter-of-factly, "So's mine, only he died a long time ago. Hey, Gary, you any good at baseball?"

"Some. I like to play."

Jimmy nodded. "Good. Come back to school on Saturday. That's when we get up a game."

The bell rang again. With a shrug and a look of resignation, Jimmy joined the children heading for the school and Gary followed him.

Inside the classroom Gary sat again at the desk that had been given him. He glanced around and now there were smiles aimed his way. Maybe a new school wouldn't be so bad after all.

By the time the dismissal bell rang, Gary was feeling at ease in his new class. He rose with the books he would need to do his homework and headed out the door. Billy Walker was leaning against a wall and he motioned Gary over when he came out.

"Hey, Gary, wanta have some fun tonight?"

Gary considered the matter, then nodded. "Doing what?" he asked.

"The moon is full tonight and we're going to bait the old witch. Wanta come along?"

"Witch? What witch?"

"Old Mama Spoonaker."

"Aw, there ain't no witches around anymore."

"Yeah? Well, Bellarosa's got one. She lives back in the woods outside of town and she's a witch for sure," Billy insisted.

"There ain't no witches," Gary repeated. "What makes you think old Mama What'sername is one?"

"It's Mama *Spoonaker*, and she has a big black cat and she can cast spells," Billy said stubbornly.

"What kind of spells?"

"She poisoned the Welker family last summer. They was all sick and almost died."

"How'd she do that?"

"Cast a spell, dummy."

Gary thought for a moment, then asked, "If she's so bad, how come you want to go bait her?"

"For fun," Billy said defiantly. "We get her riled and she chases us off. If you don't want to come, forget it."

Gary sighed. It didn't sound like much fun to him, but if he wanted to fit in he would have to go along. "I'll go, but I have to do my homework first."

"That's okay," Billy said, somewhat mollified. "We don't go 'til around midnight. We meet at the old barn on the road out of town about 11:30."

Gary stared. "My mom won't let me go out that late at night, Billy."

Billy shook his head in disgust. "Don't tell her, goofy. Wait 'til she's asleep, then sneak out a window.

She'll never know you're gone. We'll get back before morning."

"Well...okay. I'll try it this once." Gary backed away from Billy saying, "I'll see you guys later," and headed for home.

CHAPTER TWO

BAIT A WITCH?

WHEN GARY ARRIVED home his mother was unloading groceries from their car and Gary automatically accepted the bag she handed him. It was heavy, for Buttercup was no longer giving milk and there was a gallon in the sack his mother had brought from the store in Bellarosa.

"I'll sure be glad when Buttercup has her calf and we can milk her again," Mary said. "Store milk is expensive and I don't think it tastes as good, do you?"

Gary shook his head. "No, I don't, Mom. It tastes thinner or something."

She nodded. "They skim the top cream off to make butter like we do, but I guess they take more of it." Then she glanced at him and asked, "How was school, honey?"

"It was okay. My books are the same as the ones I had before." He paused, then added, "I met some of the guys."

13

"Are they friendly?"

He grinned. "Sure, Mom. You don't have to worry about me. I can make friends with anybody if they'll let me. These guys aren't much different than the ones from the other school. They already asked me to play ball with them on Saturday."

"Well, good! You're getting pale as a ghost from staying inside so much." She put the groceries on the table and turned to look at him, nodding in agreement with herself.

Gary shifted uncomfortably. He hadn't mentioned the invitation to go bait a witch that night for he knew in his heart she wouldn't approve, but he did want some friends.

"Is there such a thing as a witch, Mom?" he asked.

His mother stared at him at the abrupt change of subject, then said slowly, "I don't think so, honey. Why do you ask?"

He shrugged. "Oh-h-h, the guys were talking about an old woman who lives near here. They said she's a witch."

"Maybe they were just trying to scare you, honey. You know you're the new boy in town."

Gary made a wry face. "Well, they didn't. I ain't scared of anything like ghosts or witches." He placed the sack he was carrying on the kitchen table, then turned to face his mother. "*Is* there such a thing as a witch, Mom?"

"I don't think so," she said slowly. "I think people just thought there were at one time. Some women were even burned at the stake in Massachusetts because people thought they were casting spells and other nonsense like that."

Gary's eyes widened. *"Burned* them? Gosh, Mom, the old woman the guys were talking about cast a spell that made a family all sick last summer."

Mary shook her head. "That's probably just superstition. Usually there's a logical explanation for things like that. People just have to find the real cause. Did they? I mean, the sickness of the family. Did they find out what really caused it?"

"I don't know, Mom. The guys just said it was old Mama Spoonaker who cast the spell and that everybody knows she's a witch."

Gary returned to the car to get the rest of the groceries. He deposited the sacks on the table, then stood indecisive until his mother brushed a kiss over the top of his head.

"You'd better do your homework, honey. Don't worry about a witch. This Mrs. Spoonaker probably made the boys angry about something, so they just call her a witch. A lot of people back in old Salem accused their enemies of being witches just to get even for whatever they had quarreled about."

"And people believed them? Enough, I mean, to actually burn them at a stake?"

Mary sighed. "I'm afraid people believe what they want to believe, Gary, and it's difficult to convince them they might be wrong." She brushed his hair back from his forehead. "Now go do your homework while I put the car away and then I'll fix supper."

Gary went into the dining room and spread his books, then sat in one of the chairs and stared at them. At last he opened one and began reading. He'd think about witches when he finished his homework.

When it was time for supper, Spike took his usual place beneath the table beside Gary's knee. Even though Spike was fed liberally, Gary knew his dog liked to have some of whatever his master was eating. He slipped tidbits down to his dog at every meal while his mother pretended not to notice.

"Did you finish your homework?" she asked when the meal had ended.

"Yes, ma'am."

"I'll wash and you dry and then we'll watch television if you like."

"Okay, Mom," he said, picking up a towel.

The dishes were soon put away and the two settled down before the television set in the living room. Spike curled up on the sofa next to Gary, ignoring the frown Mary sent his way. Gary picked up the remote control unit and switched from one channel to another until at last he found one with a clear picture.

"We could get a lot more channels on the farm," he grumbled.

"That's because we had a much higher and more powerful antenna," his mother said. "The one on this house is old, so as soon as I can I'll have it replaced with a better one."

"Okay," he said, then yawned. "Gosh, I'm sleepy. Guess I'll go to bed early tonight."

"I'm ready now if you are," his mother said. "New things always make me tense and wear me out. I could sure use a good night's sleep."

Gary switched off the set and kissed his mother good-night. "See you in the morning, Mom."

He brushed his teeth as usual, but back in his room he kept his clothes on instead of getting into his pajamas. He turned off the light in case his mother looked in, but left his watch on his wrist. At intervals he squinted at it in the moonlight. He didn't want to be late for his meeting with the guys or they'd think he was a wimp.

He sighed. What if there were such a thing as a witch? If she got mad at them, could she turn them into animals or something? He shivered, then mentally shook himself. If the guys had done this "baiting" before and nothing happened to them, it probably wouldn't cause trouble tonight.

What *was* "baiting" anyhow? He knew about bait for fishing, usually worms. Were the guys going to throw worms at the old woman? Sounded silly. He sighed again and squinted at his watch. It showed only a little after ten, so he still had time to wait. Absently, he scratched Spike behind his ears, then drew him closer for comfort. He wasn't at all sure about this night's doings.

How was he going to get out of the house without his mother hearing? If he slipped downstairs and out the door, his mother would be sleeping in a house anybody could enter. And Spike. He eyed his dog thoughtfully. Should he take Spike along? If he didn't, his dog would probably raise a racket and wake his mother. Maybe he and Spike could go out one of the living-room windows and close it behind them. There were lots of bushes around the house and so it wouldn't be easy for a burglar to test the windows.

When eleven o'clock finally rolled around, Gary quietly opened his door and peeked out. The house was dark, so his mother was probably asleep. With a cautioning "shhh" to Spike, he tiptoed into the hall and down the stairs with Spike on his heels. One of the stairs squeaked as he stepped on it and Gary held his breath for a moment, wondering if his mother had heard. When she didn't come out to look, he went on, carefully planting his weight at the side of the steps where they were firmest.

In the living room he quietly opened a window, lifted Spike through, then climbed out. Spike whined when the branches on the shrubbery pulled at his coat. Gary grunted as they scratched at his hands and face and hung on his clothing, but he ducked his head and scrambled through the thicket. Then he remembered he had forgotten to close the window, and had to get scratched again as he returned to close it and then get out again to where Spike waited. He licked at a small scratch on one hand that began to ooze blood, then shoved it into his pocket and walked into the night.

The moon gave enough light to see around him, but it also made everything have shadows and look spooky. Spike trotted along beside him, glancing up every so often as if to ask why they were outside at this time of night instead of snug in bed.

"It's okay, boy," Gary whispered. "We're going to meet the guys and have some fun." He sighed, then added, "I hope."

The old barn loomed ahead in the moonlight and

soon Gary saw the guys hunkered down beside it as they waited for him. Billy rose when he saw Gary and the others followed suit.

"We thought you weren't coming," Billy said.

"Aw, I knew he'd be here," Jimmy said. "He said he would and he's no quitter."

"'Course I'm not," Gary answered indignantly. "I always keep my word and it's just now 11:30."

"Why'd you bring your dog?" Willie asked. "He'll give us away."

"If I left him he'd make a racket. He knows I'm not s'posed to be out this late."

"Well, let's get going," Billy said. "Nobody talk from now on, and keep that dog quiet."

The boys walked down a lane into deeper woods where the trees kept the ground shaded from the moon. In the quiet of the night Gary heard strange noises. He tried to see around him but all he could see were various shades of shadows. His skin began to feel crawly. Sleepy chirpings came from the trees and in the distance a frog croaked at the moon. Dead leaves crackled when he walked over them and Gary wished he were home.

Soon Billy stopped and motioned the others to squat down beside him. "We're close enough," he whispered. "Now gather all the rocks you can find and we'll scare the old witch out of bed."

"You mean we're going to throw rocks at her?" Gary asked, and there was a dubious note in his lowered voice.

"Naw, stupid," Billy whispered. "We'll throw them at her house and start yelling at the same time. Maybe she'll think we're Indians come back from the

dead." He snickered. "Last time she came out screeching and waving a broom."

Jimmy stifled a snicker, saying, "She sure looked
funny."

It sounded dumb to Gary, but if he wanted to fit in
with his classmates, he'd have to go along. Slowly,
he gathered several pebbles, then returned to the
others.

"The house is in the clearing just over there," Billy
said, gesturing with his elbow because his hands
were full of rocks. "Let's go."

The five boys moved silently through the trees
until they reached the edge of a clearing. In the
center of the clearing was a small frame house
surrounded by shrubbery and a few shade trees.
Not a light showed. Not a creature stirred. The
moon outlined the house as though it were in a
spotlight.

"Now!" Billy said.

The boys ran into the clearing yelling like Indians
and throwing rocks at the small cottage. Gary ran
with them, but he dropped the pebbles he had gathered.
Spike romped along at his master's heels, as usual,
and added barking to the general din. It was as
though a riot had suddenly erupted in the quiet
moonlit night. Then the sound of shattering glass
echoed in the clearing and lights came on inside the
cottage.

Abruptly, a huge bird rose from one of the sheltering
trees and flew swiftly toward the group. With an
ear-splitting screech the owl swooped down on the
boys. Willie was just in front of Gary and the bird
flogged his head with his huge wings and left a talon

cut somewhere for Willie shrieked with pain and covered his face with his hands.

Then the dreadful creature was on Gary and he felt a talon rip his cheek before the hateful wings took the owl away. With a yelp of pain Gary dropped to the ground, pulling Spike under his arm before he covered his head with his hands.

Then another mind-freezing screech filled the air and Gary scrunched closer to the ground, shivering with fear. Spike tried to loosen himself, but Gary took one hand from his head and clutched him tighter. He didn't want his dog trying to fight a creature such as this.

The Indian yells of the other boys changed to cries of terror as they turned and fled toward the cover of the surrounding woods, dragging Willie with them.

Gary heard them retreating and knew they had left him alone. He lay frozen on the ground, then cautiously raised his head so he could look around. Spike stood up, licking anxiously at the bleeding scratch on his master's cheek. The owl must have followed the guys, for Gary heard a distant screech. He rose... and then his heart stood still!

Coming toward him from the cottage was a black ball of fur with great yellow eyes glaring and an open mouth spitting yowls such as Gary had never heard. Behind the fury was an old woman clad in black robes fluttering in the breeze. She was standing on the porch and flourishing a cane, screeching almost like the owl.

The fur on Spike's neck stood up as he bared his teeth at the approaching menace.

"Come on, boy!" Gary yelled, then turned and fled toward the woods.

With a reluctant look back at the nearing challenger, Spike obeyed and bounded after Gary. When they reached the woods, Gary looked back and saw the big cat had stopped following them, although his fur was still standing straight out and his mouth still emitted howls that curdled Gary's blood.

"You don't want to fight him, Spike," he said, then walked through the woods as fast as he could. Spike's hair was still on end but he obediently followed. That was the trouble with Spike, Gary decided. He just never knew when to leave trouble alone. Neither do I, he thought despondently. That shattering glass must have been a window and that meant real trouble. Why had he done a dumb thing like going with the guys tonight? He knew the answer—he wanted to fit in with his new classmates. He groaned. If he had to do dumb things like this to get them to accept him, maybe it wasn't worth it. Mom had been telling him lately that it was better to say no to things you knew were wrong even if your friends urged you to do them. As usual she was probably right.

Gary trudged down the path to the barn with Spike beside him. Spike gradually lowered his neck hair and stopped the rumbling deep in his throat. He looked up at Gary questioningly a time or two, but when no command was given, he stayed at Gary's side.

Nobody was at the barn when they arrived. The guys must have scattered to go home, so Gary plodded on. When they reached home Gary went through the bushes again, wincing as they tore at him, then opened the window quietly. He boosted Spike through the opening, then climbed inside and closed the window and locked it. His heart was thudding so loudly he decided it was best to wait before he went upstairs. If it sounded as loud to his mother as it sounded to him, it would wake her for sure.

He slid down the wall to the carpet and sat there with one hand on Spike. When his breathing again became normal and the pounding in his ears lessened, Gary decided to try for his room. As silently as possible, he climbed the stairs, stepping over the one that had tried to give him away before.

Once inside his room, he looked in a mirror at his face and closed his eyes in despair. The cut had stopped bleeding but there was no way he could hide it from his mother in the morning. He spit on his handkerchief and dabbed at the blood, carefully so as not to start it bleeding again. He should wash it, but if he went to the bathroom he might wake his mother and that was something he would rather not do.

With a sigh, Gary dropped his clothing in a heap, put on his pajamas and climbed into bed. Spike licked at the cut on his master's face and Gary let him continue. Dogs healed their own wounds by licking them and maybe Spike could fix the talon slash. At least it didn't burn as badly as before.

Then Spike nestled up close to him, but Gary turned away and curled into a ball. He was aching in places he hadn't noticed in the past, and he worried about what to tell his mother.

Now he had seen a witch! In his mind's eye he could still see the old woman clad in black and her big black cat coming at him with a mouth that was all teeth. Her big old owl had flogged heads and scratched faces and screeched in a way to freeze your blood. Gary's head still ached like the rest of his body, but there was nothing he could do about it now. Hoping he wouldn't dream about the creatures he had seen, he closed his eyes and went to sleep.

CHAPTER THREE

PAYMENT DUE

WHEN GARY WOKE he felt as though he had just fallen asleep. As usual, Spike knew when it was time to get up, for he was licking at his master's ear with a rough tongue. With a sigh, Gary brushed him away and sat up.

He dreaded the meeting with his mother. How could he explain the cut on his face that hadn't been there when she kissed him good-night? It was no use making up some dumb story for she always saw through it. Reluctantly, he rose and dressed himself in clean clothing, then gathered up the dirty ones from his night expedition and crammed them into the hamper in the bathroom. After brushing his teeth and examining the cut that wouldn't wash away, he made himself walk down the stairs to meet his mother.

She was not in the kitchen. Gary let Spike out the door, then went looking for her in the other rooms. She was nowhere to be seen. He heard Spike barking out near the shed and went to investigate.

Inside the shed, Mary was sitting on a bale of hay watching a newborn calf trying to find her mother's milk.

"Calves are so awkward when they've just been born," she said with a glance in Gary's direction. "I'll have to stay here until she begins to nurse. Can you fix your breakfast this morning, honey?"

"Hey, it's a heifer!" Gary exclaimed. "That's great, but how come she doesn't look like Buttercup?"

"The father was a red and white Hereford and Buttercup is a Jersey. This baby happens to take after the father."

Gary nodded, careful to keep his injured cheek away from his mother's eyes. "I can fix my breakfast, Mom. See you after school."

Mary kept her eyes on the calf as she held her face up for Gary's kiss. He hastily brushed one across her cheek, then returned to the house with Spike trailing behind him.

"Mustn't bother the calf, boy," he said to his dog.

The knot in his stomach had dissolved when he realized his mother was too busy to notice his injuries. After school maybe he could just say he fell or something. Was a white lie about something like that as bad as a whopping big lie about something important? He could ask Dad if he were here. Dad had always been willing to talk about it when Gary had goofed. Then he would figure out Gary's best course of action.

Gary glanced at the clock, then hurriedly ate his breakfast and headed for school. The bell was just ringing as he reached the schoolyard so at least he wouldn't be late for class.

Billy was inside, as were the other guys. Willie had a big patch on his face where the owl had gouged him and he looked miserable. His mother had probably given him what-for. John and Jimmy looked okay but Billy shook his head at Gary when he caught his eye. Maybe the story wouldn't get out if they all acted as though nothing had happened. At least Gary hoped so.

It was a vain hope. Just before recess, a big man dressed in khaki and with a bright star on his chest came into the classroom and said something in a low voice to the teacher. Gary's heart sank. He scrunched lower in his seat and hoped he wouldn't be noticed.

"Billy Walker, stand up," the man ordered. "Now you all know I'm Sheriff Ben Thompson and I have a complaint about a broken window from Mrs. Spoonaker. She recognized you, Billy, but there were others with you last night. Who were they?"

Billy shrugged. "I was home in bed last night, sheriff. I don't know what you're talking about." He sat down.

"I told you to stand up, Billy," Sheriff Thompson said, then waited until Billy reluctantly rose to his feet again. "Now Mrs. Spoonaker identified you as one of a bunch of boys who broke her window last night. Who were the others?"

When Billy said nothing, the sheriff looked around the room until he came to Willie. "Willie Haus, it looks as though you tangled with something just recently. It couldn't have been Mrs. Spoonaker's pet owl, now could it?"

"Yes, sir," Willie mumbled, rising to his feet. "I'm real sorry about the whole thing."

Sheriff Thompson frowned as he said, "At least you aren't lying, Willie, and that's in your favor. Now you tell me who else was at the party."

With a sigh, Gary rose and stood facing the sheriff. "I was there," he said. "I'm sure sorry about the whole business too."

The sheriff went over and examined Gary's cut cheek. "Looks like you could use some first aid, son. When we finish here you had better go see the school nurse and have that cut tended to."

Then he looked around the class again, saying, "There were five of you, so the other two better admit they were there."

Jimmy Allen and John James slid out of their seats and stood with downcast eyes beside their desks.

"Well, you fellows really made a mess last night, didn't you?" the sheriff said. "What's wrong with you—teasing a ninety-year-old woman like that? You not only scared her, you broke the expensive bay window where she grows herbs."

"Aw, she's a witch," Billy said. "Everybody knows that."

The sheriff shook his head in disgust. "They do, do they? I don't know that. I know she's a lonely old woman that you kids devil from time to time and I want it stopped. This time you did some serious damage and either you or your parents will have to pay. It will cost $200 to replace that window! Divided by five, that adds up to $40 from each of you."

Gary's eyes widened. That was a lot of money! He wanted to help his mother, not cost her.

"Where we gonna get money like that?" Billy asked.

"Well, Mrs. Spoonaker can't do much for herself

anymore. She said you could each work it out if you want."

"I ain't gonna work for no witch," Billy said defiantly. "My dad won't pay her, either. She can just spell her window fixed!"

"I ain't gonna work for her either," John and Jimmy said as though one breath.

"I'm scared of her," Willie whimpered. "My ma already gave me a licking. Ain't that enough?"

Sheriff Thompson shook his head. "No, it isn't. Either you boys go chore for her until she says you're paid or your folks will have to give Mrs. Spoonaker money for a new window." His eyes fell on Gary. "You're the new kid, aren't you? How come you're already mixed up in something like this?"

"Yes, sir, I'm new," Gary answered, his voice cracking on the last word. Then in a whisper he added, "Guess I'm just dumb!"

The sheriff nodded. "Well, you boys decide whether you will work it out or get your folks to pay. New boy, what's your name?"

"Gary Benson."

"Well, get yourself to the nurse before that cut festers. Then either report to Mrs. Spoonaker after school or tell your folks you have to pay forty dollars."

Sheriff Thompson left and Miss Black dismissed Gary so he could see the nurse. Gary hurried from the room, his mind racing around the consequence of last night's "fun." No way would he tell his mother about any forty dollars! He would go work out his part. The old woman had sure looked fierce standing on the porch waving a stick last night! The big cat and that old owl were nothing to fool with either, but he still didn't quite believe the old woman was a witch. Or was she? Either way, he would go work for her. Dad always said to stand up and fess up when you were wrong, so maybe if he told Mrs. Spoonaker he was sorry and would work at whatever she wanted him to do, she would keep her old owl and cat from attacking him.

After the school nurse had doctored his cut and covered it with a Band-Aid, Gary returned to class. Recess was over and the guys didn't look too happy, but they tended to their books for the rest of the day and at lunch all any of them would say was that they were not about to go near any old witch again.

"We ain't gonna pay and we ain't gonna work for the old hag," Billy said, and the others nodded in agreement. "How about you, Gary?"

"Guess I'll go work it out," Gary answered.

"Ain't you scared?" Willie asked.

"Sure, I'm scared," Gary said, "but if I work for her maybe she won't turn me into a toad or something."

"Aw, that's dumb," Billy said with a sneer, but the others looked at Gary with a sort of respect in their eyes.

When Gary reached home, the first thing his mother noticed was the bandage on his face.

"What happened to your face, honey?" she asked. "Here, let me take a look." Carefully, she lifted the bandage and peered at the jagged cut underneath. "That looks awful, Gary. How did it happen?"

Miserably, Gary shifted from one foot to the other, trying to decide between a lie and the truth. Then with a sigh, he decided the truth would have to come out if he were going to work for Mrs. Spoonaker every day after school.

"Well, Mom," he said slowly, "an old owl scratched me."

"Wha-at?"

Then the truth came rushing out of Gary's mouth as he told her of last night's escapade, but he looked at the floor while he was telling it.

Mary put her hand under his chin and gently raised his head so he would have to look at her.

"Gosh, I'm sorry, Mom!" he blurted. "I'll have to work for Mrs. Spoonaker for awhile to pay for my part of her window. I have to go see her now." Then he hesitated before adding, "Do *you* think she's a witch, Mom?"

Mary went to the refrigerator and poured a glass of milk, then set the glass and the cookie jar on the table. "You had better eat something before you go, Gary, just in case you're late for supper," she said, seating herself at the table across from him. "I hope she doesn't keep you out there after dark."

"You didn't answer, Mom. *Is* the old woman a witch?"

"I don't know Mrs. Spoonaker, Gary, but I don't think she's a witch. If she is, she's ninety years old and she surely doesn't have much power anymore. Otherwise she could do her own chores, couldn't she? Or have her cat or something do them with a flick of her hand?"

Gary thought about it for a time, then said in a low voice, "Are you gonna punish me for sneaking out last night, Mom?"

Tears came into her eyes as she said, "I wish your father were here."

"So do I, Mom."

Then she blinked back her tears and said, "No, I think you'll be punished enough by working out what you owe. Oh, Gary, I hope you won't be so ready to go along with things like this that your friends want you to do. And I hope that cut on your cheek doesn't leave a scar. That big owl might have killed you, you know. Owls are predators. I didn't think they would attack people, but perhaps Mrs. Spoonaker taught this one to protect her when idiots come around."

Gary looked sheepish as he said, "Like me?" Then he rose. "I'd better get going, Mom. I'll be home as soon as I finish and I'll do my homework then. I'll milk Buttercup, too."

"Buttercup is busy with her calf and her milk won't be fit to use for at least three days. Be careful, honey, and mind your manners. Even an over-the-hill witch might be dangerous," she said, but a twinkle in her eye belied her belief in witches.

Gary hugged her. "You're a good old mom," he said. "I'll be good, don't worry. Will you keep Spike here so he doesn't tangle with that cat?"

Mary laughed as she brushed a kiss across his head. "I'll keep Spike here in the kitchen to protect me until you get back. Ask her to please not keep you too late, okay?"

Gary left and walked the distance to the old barn and then down the path to the cottage in the clearing. As he neared his destination his feet slowed down, but then he raised his chin and marched firmly onward over the path and up to Mrs. Spoonaker's door.

He glanced fearfully around, but no owl swooped from a tree, no cat came spitting and yowling. Gently, Gary knocked on the door.

Soon it opened and Gary looked up at a wrinkled old woman leaning on a cane. She was dressed in black again, but this time a white apron was tied around her waist.

"Well, what is it, young man?" she asked impatiently.

Gary swallowed the lump that had risen in his throat, then said, "I'm Gary Benson, Mrs. Spoonaker. I didn't break your window but I was with the boys who did and I've come to do chores for you to pay for my part. I have to do forty dollars' worth."

"Humph!" she said, frowning fiercely. "You young rascals have deviled me for the last time. I need my sleep, not the bedlam you young hooligans raised last night."

"Yes'm. I am real sorry it happened, ma'am, and I'll sure never do it again."

"Well, come in, come in and we'll talk about it," she said, turning and limping painfully toward a chair by the big fireplace.

Gary followed her, then stood waiting, almost afraid to move. The big black cat was curled up on the hearth sleeping and Gary sure didn't want to wake him.

"Well, sit down, sit down," the old woman said. "You say your name is Gary?"

He nodded.

"Well, Gary, are you afraid of me?"

"Sort of," Gary said cautiously. "Is your owl around today?"

"Did he do that to your cheek?"

"Yes'm."

The old woman sighed. "Well, he isn't really *my* owl. I found him after he had fallen out of a nest in one of the trees. He wasn't feathered out yet so I took him in and fed him until he could fly. He comes back to visit but he isn't a pet." She looked at Gary and when he said nothing, added, "Fu only goes on the attack when he thinks I'm in danger. You were unlucky enough to come screaming on a night he had chosen to visit. I'm sorry about your face."

"Is that his name—Fu?"

She chuckled, although it came out more of a cackle, then said, "Well, I had to call him something. Fu stands for Fu Yin or Fu On You—whichever is appropriate at the time."

Despite his fear, Gary had to smile. Mrs. Spoonaker wasn't nearly so fierce as he had imagined she would be, and she even joked!

"Now, young man, about your chores," she said in a business tone of voice. "Can you mow a lawn with a push mower? Are you strong enough?"

"Oh, sure, I can do that," Gary answered. "Do you want me to start now?"

"Do you go to school?"

"Yes'm."

"Do you have homework to do?"

"Yes'm."

"Do you have chores to do for your parents in the afternoon?"

"I help my mother. My father is dead."

The old woman peered closely into Gary's face, then nodded as though satisfied with what she saw. "I think you'll do, Gary Benson. However, I think you'll do chores for me on Saturday instead of every day after school. Depends on how you work how long it will take to earn forty dollars, but we'll see, we'll see. Will Saturday be all right with you?"

"Oh, yes, ma'am, Saturday will be fine. Can I help you with anything today?"

"No, we'll wait until Saturday. Come early and tell your mother I would like to meet her when she has time. I can't get out and around very much, but if she'll come visit me, I would appreciate it."

"Yes, ma'am, I'll do just that," Gary said. "Should I leave now?"

She nodded. "You'll have to go back the way you came unless you want a ride on my broomstick."

Gary's eyes widened at her words and then he gulped and said, "Oh, no, thanks, ma'am, I'll just walk. I'll go back home the way I came."

He backed away until one foot touched the door, then he hastily opened it and fled down the path. He could have sworn he heard a cackling laugh as he ran!

CHAPTER
FOUR

BROOMSTICKS AND SADDLES

GARY STOPPED RUNNING at the old barn and paused to catch his breath. If the old woman could really ride a broomstick she was a witch! Then his imagination came alive and he wondered how it would feel to fly through the air with just a broomstick holding you up there. Maybe when he knew Mrs. Spoonaker better she would offer again and then he would find out. He would ride on her broomstick if she showed him how!

His breathing and heartbeat returned to normal and Gary trudged homeward, pondering his visit with the witch. She seemed okay after he had apologized. Helping her with chores wouldn't be so bad. He grinned at the memory of her joke about the owl. She was old, but anybody who would joke with him after he had been part of last night's devilment couldn't be all bad. Her cat had slept through their meeting, so perhaps he wasn't all that vicious after all. Gary's spirits were high.

Then he sobered. If he was working for Mrs. Spoonaker on Saturdays he would miss the ball games Jimmy had mentioned. He squared his shoulders and resolved to work as hard as he could so his forty dollars' worth wouldn't take too long. Then he could play in the games. He sighed. No matter what he did these days, things just didn't go right. Wish Dad were still here, he thought dismally. Dad had always straightened things out for him when he was jammed up.

When Gary walked into the kitchen, Spike jumped up to greet him and Gary's mother gave him a hug and a kiss.

"Finish your work so early?" she asked. "Mrs. Spoonaker must be pretty nice."

"I'm going to work for her on Saturdays, Mom. She asked me if I had homework and chores and when I said I had, she said Saturdays would be okay."

"There, you see? She isn't as bad as you thought, is she?"

Gary grinned. "Naw, she's not as scary as I thought, but she's probably a witch. She offered me a ride on her broomstick if I wanted one."

Mary laughed, then said, "She was probably putting you on, honey. She most likely knows people around here call her a witch so she was teasing."

"Maybe," Gary said doubtfully. "Anyhow, if she offers again I think I'll go. She told me to ask you to come visit her when you have time 'cause she can't get around much anymore, so will you?"

Mary nodded. "I'll phone her this week and see what day is convenient. I might even ask to see her license for flying a broomstick."

"Now *you're* pulling my leg, Mom. You don't believe in witches, but this time you might be wrong."

His mother smiled, saying, "Better go do your homework so you'll be caught up if the broomstick crashes."

"C'mon, Spike," Gary said. They trudged up the stairs to his room together. Maybe there weren't any witches, but that old woman was awfully spooky at times.

During the next few days Gary learned the names of the rest of the boys, and took a lot of kidding from them. Even the girls joined in the general teasing as they asked him to bring them love potions from Mama Spoonaker's kettle. Heather Johnson, however, was more concerned. After she told Gary her name, she went into the subject of the witch.

"Aren't you scared to go out there?" she asked, her eyes wide. "I'm afraid of Mama Spoonaker. The first time I saw her she was walking down the sidewalk and she glared at me as she passed." Then she added, "Of course that was a long time ago, when I was little."

Gary smiled at the dark-haired little girl. "I'm scared of her old owl and that big black cat, but I don't think Mrs. Spoonaker is so awful."

Heather sighed in admiration. "You're so brave, Gary! All the other boys are afraid to go near her and their folks will have to pay their share of the window."

Gary's chest swelled as a good feeling filled him. "Aw, it's nothing," he said modestly. "I just didn't want my mother to have to pay for what I did."

"That Billy Walker is the biggest fool I know!" Heather said indignantly. "He's always getting into trouble and getting everybody else in trouble, too. How come you joined his old gang?"

"I didn't know I was joining any gang," Gary said slowly. "I just thought it was nice that some of the guys were so friendly when I just got here."

"Well... I guess it really isn't a gang," Heather admitted, "but he's always getting Willie and the others into some dumb scrape. Mr. Dickens expelled Billy from school once, but his folks are rich and they made Mr. Dickens let him come back." She sighed wistfully. "I wish my folks were rich."

"Why?"

"So I could have some shoe skates. My mother says we can't afford things like that."

Gary nodded as he said, "I know what you mean. My mother wants me to go to college and that costs a lot of money, so I don't even ask for anything I don't really need."

"Well, if you get Mama Spoonaker to like you, maybe she will get you things you want with one of her spells."

Gary laughed. "I'll be lucky if she doesn't turn me into a toad," he said.

Heather ran back to her friends and Gary walked toward the gate and home. It was Friday and in the morning he would have to get up early to walk all the way to the Spoonaker place. Since no homework was given to be done during the weekends, at least he didn't have that to worry about.

As he neared the yard to his home, he noticed a saddled pony tied to the fence beside the gate. He quickened his pace and looked curiously at the pony before he went up the walk and into the kitchen.

"Do we have company, Mom?" he asked.

Mary was sitting alone in the kitchen darning a sock. She shook her head as she said, "Only Jock and he's going to stay with us for awhile."

"Who's Jock?"

"The pony outside. You passed him when you came in, didn't you?"

"You bought me a pony?" Gary asked incredulously. "How come, Mom?"

"No, I didn't buy you a pony," Mary said patiently. "I met Mr. Kurlacher in the store today. He delivers honey from his bees when the store needs a supply. While we were talking, he said his son had outgrown his pony and he wanted to pass it along to a boy who would take good care of him, and when he outgrew Jock, pass the outfit along to a smaller boy with the same conditions. When he asked if you would do that, I said you sure would."

"Gosh, Mom, that's great! I'll take real good care of him." He paused, then a smile lit up his face. "Hey, I'll be able to ride out to Spoonaker's and back and it won't take near as long."

"I think that's why Mr. Kurlacher made the offer," his mother said gently. "Since you were the only boy willing to work out the damage that was done, he feels you'll be responsible enough to care for Jock. Only... Gary, you have never ridden a pony before. Do you think you can?"

"Sure, Mom, what's to know? You just get on and go and use the reins to steer with, just like the guys on television do. Can I go try him now?"

"Change your sneaks for those boots that came with the outfit and then you may. Mr. Kurlacher said it's better to wear boots when you ride and these are still in good shape."

Gary unlaced his sneakers and slipped into the boots. When he rose and walked around, the bootheels clicked on the floor. "They're sort of big, Mom, but they'll do. All cowboys wear boots," he said. The heels sort of pushed him forward but he'd get used to them.

His mother laughed. "At least they make you taller. Be careful with that pony. Mr. Kurlacher said Jock hadn't been ridden in a long time and ponies get wild when they aren't used frequently."

Gary grinned as they headed outside. How many times had he wished he were a cowboy as he watched them on television? It would be nicer to have a horse, but a pony was okay. Could a pony travel as fast as a horse? He would have to find out.

When Gary and his mother reached the spot where Jock stood, the pony was nibbling at the shrubbery just inside the fence. Gary untied the reins and slipped them over the pony's head while his mother stood ready to help him. Spike had followed them and now he sat down, his head cocked to one side as though trying to figure out what this was all about.

"I won't need any help, Mom," Gary said. "This old pony is tame. Good Jock," he said, patting the pony's neck.

"Want me to give you a boost on?" Mary asked.

"I ain't a baby, Mom. I've watched lots of cowboys get on their horses and nobody boosts them."

He put a foot into one stirrup and began to swing his leg over to the other side when the saddle turned upside down and dumped him on the ground. Jock looked around, still chewing on some leaves.

"Gary, are you all right?" his mother asked as she hurried to help him up. "Oh, dear, I forgot Mr. Kurlacher loosened the saddle. He said it should be taken off when you aren't riding Jock, but he left it on so you could just tighten it."

Gary scrambled to his feet, his pride shaken. "I should have remembered it myself, Mom. A cowboy always tightens his cinch before he gets on."

He boosted the saddle and blanket back into place on Jock's back and this time tightened the cinch that held it firm. "Now we'll see about this," he muttered as he pulled himself astride.

"Giddyup," he said to the back of Jock's head.

The pony flicked his tail and moved his ears, but his feet stayed firmly planted.

"How do I make him go, Mom?"

Mary shook her head. "I have never been on a horse so I don't know. Perhaps if you nudged him in the ribs with your bootheels..."

Gary nodded. He touched Jock's ribs with his boots, then kicked harder when the pony still didn't move. "Giddyup," he repeated loudly, then kicked again.

This time Jock moved. His ears flattened against his head and he took off in a gallop that nearly unseated his small rider.

"Whoa, boy!" Gary shouted, clutching the horn on the saddle to keep from falling off. "Slow down!"

Suddenly Jock stopped, but Gary didn't. Leaving his boots in the stirrups, Gary sailed over the pony's head and landed on his back in front of Jock. With the breath knocked out of him and the sky spinning dizzily above, Gary struggled to get some air and was still unable to speak when his mother reached him and stooped to gather him into her arms.

"Oh, Gary, are you all right?" she asked, then rubbed his back hard in an attempt to help him regain his breath.

Spike had run to where Gary lay and was frantically licking any part of his face that he could reach. Mary brushed him away.

"Oh, why did I let Mr. Kurlacher give me that miserable beast!" she wailed. "He's liable to kill you!"

"Ulp mmm ah," Gary whispered, then sat up and took several deep breaths before he tried to speak again. "I'm okay, Mom," he said weakly. "I just wasn't expecting him to stop so suddenly." The sky had stopped spinning but his whole body ached from being slammed against the ground.

"Well, I am going to return that animal to Mr. Kurlacher first thing tomorrow," Mary said indignantly. "He can just give him to somebody else!"

"Oh no, Mom, don't do that. I'll learn how to ride him, you'll see. You won't really take him back, will you?"

"Oh, honey, I just can't lose you, too. I couldn't bear it," she whispered as tears filled her eyes.

"Aw, Mom, you won't lose me," Gary said, giving her a hug. "I might lose my boots, but I'll get 'em back," he added, trying to make her smile.

He patted Spike on the head to make up for his mother pushing him away. "I'm okay, boy," he said, and Spike rose and wagged his tail.

Gary rose from where he had fallen, trying not to groan as his back let him know it had been hurt. He grinned as he approached Jock and removed his boots from the stirrups. "I'll ride you yet, you old pony," he muttered. "Now I know you're a stopper I'll be more careful."

Mary watched as he put on his boots and again began to mount the pony. She started to say something, then pressed her lips together. If Bob were still alive he would want his son to try again. Her anxious eyes followed Gary's movements as he seated himself in the saddle and slipped his feet into the stirrups.

With one hand clutching the horn of the saddle and the other holding the reins, Gary said, "Giddyup, you old goat," and clapped his heels into the pony's sides.

Jock sprang forward and tried to take off in a run, but this time Gary pulled the reins so tight the pony's chin almost touched his chest and Jock slowed to a stop.

"Do it right, dummy," Gary muttered, then said, "Giddyup," once more.

This time Jock moved forward at a walk and Gary wheeled the animal around to face his mother.

"See, Mom? I can handle him."

With that, Jock gave a wild leap sideways and began to buck. This time Gary was ready for him, for he hadn't watched all those westerns on television for nothing. With his knees clamped tightly against the pony's sides and still hanging onto the saddle horn, Gary stayed with the bucking pony. This time the sky jumped around and the earth wavered back and forth and his back hurt like the dickens, but he kept a death grip on Jock while his backside rose from the saddle, then thumped back down against it.

Mary pressed her fists into her mouth so she wouldn't cry out and silently prayed for her son as the pony gyrated wildly around in a circle.

Jock soon tired of his efforts when he failed to unseat his rider. He stopped, his sides heaving and foam flecking his coat. Then he turned his head to look at Gary and snorted between pantings.

"He's saying I won!" Gary said triumphantly. He slid from the pony's back, this time with his boots still on his feet. He patted the pony's sweaty neck and rubbed the velvet nose. "We're gonna be friends, Mom," he declared.

"I guess I believe you," Mary said weakly. Then as she took a deep breath, added, "But I certainly am going to talk to Mr. Kurlacher. He should have told me that pony bucks!"

Gary led Jock to where his mother stood and put his arm around her. "Aw, he ain't so wild, Mom. He probably was just trying to find out how much he could get away with. When I was a little kid, I did the same thing, didn't I?"

His mother nodded. "I'm not so sure you aren't still doing it. You know you shouldn't have sneaked out the night you did, don't you?"

"Aw, Mom, I already said I was sorry. I won't do it again. Next time I'm invited somewhere I'll ask if you want to go along," he said with a grin.

"You are just like your father," Mary said. "He would always kid his way out of messes, too," but she smiled as she said it. "Now, go unsaddle that beast and turn him into the stall next to Buttercup's and feed him. Mr. Kurlacher left a sack of feed for him in the shed. It might be better not to turn him out into the lot with Buttercup until they get acquainted."

"Okay, Mom. I'll have a long talk with that old pony," Gary promised. "I'll tell him just what he can and can't do, okay?"

"While you're having that talk, why not give him a brushing? Mr. Kurlacher left a curry comb and brush that he's been using. Ponies like that."

Gary grinned. "He's so fat and shiny now I don't think he needs much brushing, but I'll tickle him with the comb and make him giggle."

"There you go again," his mother said, shaking her head. "Supper will be ready by the time you finish if you don't take too long."

Gary looked back and saw her still watching as he led Jock into the small shed. The smile had faded from his face and he swallowed a groan that tried to emerge from his mouth. He hadn't told his mother how much his back hurt from being slammed into the ground or how sore he was all over from Jock's antics, but then Dad wouldn't have told either.

CHAPTER FIVE

"OH, MY ACHING BACK!"

THROUGHOUT SUPPER AND the evening's television, Gary's body grew stiffer and sorer. He squirmed uncomfortably, but no position he tried eased his discomfort. When bedtime arrived he could barely drag himself upstairs without groaning. He gritted his teeth and refused to utter a sound.

Then just before he climbed into bed his mother came into his room with a bottle. "Lay on your tummy, honey. This liniment should take away some of the pain in your back," she said. "Your other soreness will probably ease by morning."

Gary stared at her, then rolled onto his stomach with a groan. How had she known? It was spooky sometimes how his mother knew what was going on even when nobody told her.

Mary raised his pajama top and rubbed the soothing liquid into his back and shoulders, then massaged it until some of the aching ceased.

"Feeling better?" she asked.

"Yeah, Mom," he said with a sigh and he shifted again to his back. "How did you know my back hurt so much?"

"Well, I don't think any back that met the ground with such force could help hurting," she answered. "A fall such as you took just naturally makes you sore all over. Your father never would admit anything hurt, either, so I'm used to reading the signs."

"That stuff sure helped, Mom," he said with a grin. "Thanks."

Mary lightly kissed his forehead, then said, "You get some sleep now and I'll give you another rubdown in the morning."

He smiled sleepily and heard her soft, "Good night," as she left the room. Moms were sure nice to have around, he thought as Spike curled up next to him. It wasn't long until both pairs of eyes closed.

The next morning after his mother had again rubbed liniment into his back, the soreness was still with him but the stiffness had disappeared. Gary dressed, grateful he could walk without gritting his teeth, although he was careful about how he put anything on his back. He would be able to work for Mrs. Spoonaker as he had promised.

He was going to ride Jock out to the old woman's place, but he tied his sneaks together to hang around the saddle horn so he could change when he got there. Cowboy boots looked nice on television and were good for hanging in stirrups and protecting toes from hooves, but they sure weren't the most comfortable things to work in.

At the breakfast table his mother asked him if he were sure he could work.

"Sure, Mom. My back's just a little sore now and maybe exercise would help. Besides, I think the old woman just wants me to push her lawn mower and that's easy."

Mary nodded. "I phoned Mrs. Spoonaker yesterday and she invited me to have lunch with her today. You, too. I just have to pick up some groceries for her before I go."

"That's great, Mom. See? I said you'd be invited to go with me next time." He smiled and there was an impish twinkle in his eyes. "Maybe you can find out if she has a licence for her old broom."

His mother laughed, a sound that was like music to Gary's ears. If he could make her laugh every so often, maybe she wouldn't be so sad. He missed his father, too, but it was no use moping around about it.

"While I'm cutting grass, you can case the joint and find out what you can about the old woman," Gary added.

"Don't call her that, Gary," his mother said, suddenly sobering. "Mrs. Spoonaker is old and probably lonelier than either of us, so be nice to her."

"Okay, Mom. Now I'd better get going."

Spike wagged his tail to be taken along, but Gary said, "Sit!" and left him in the kitchen. He didn't want his dog to be clawed by that old cat.

He went out and rattled a bucket of oats to lure Jock close enough to catch. While the pony ate, Gary saddled him and slipped the bridle over his head. Then he put the bucket back in the shed and untied Jock before he climbed into the saddle.

"No rough stuff today, boy," he said sternly. "I have to work."

Jock must have agreed for he traveled easily and quickly over the road to the cottage in the clearing. At first Gary bounced with every step the pony took, but then he got into the rhythm of Jock's gait and sat firmly in the saddle. Even going to work was fun when he could ride, Gary thought. He gently nudged his heels into Jock's sides and was rewarded with a swift gallop that made the wind whistle by his ears.

When Gary was dismounting in front of the cottage, Mrs. Spoonaker hobbled out onto the porch.

"Good morning," she said, then, "Don't tie your pony there. Take him around back to the old barn and put him in the corral after you take off his saddle. It's better for him, you know."

"Yes'm," Gary agreed and did as he was told.

When he returned to the cottage, Mrs. Spoonaker was sitting on the porch. She gestured toward the side of the house. "You'll find the mower in the shed, Gary. Mow as much as you can before lunch and then put it back where you found it."

"Yes'm."

Gary pushed the mower around the cottage and then in ever-widening circles while the shaggy grass was turned into a smooth lawn. He liked the smell of cut grass and as the sun passed higher in the sky, the soreness in his back dissolved. He had changed from his boots to his sneaks when he unsaddled Jock, so walking along pushing a mower wasn't really hard work. His mind wandered as he continued to mow.

Mrs. Spoonaker looked just like any other very old woman, he decided. Did witches look like everybody else? She wasn't wearing a peaked hat like pictures showed and she didn't have snaggled teeth. Her teeth were even and white, probably false, but most old people wore false teeth. Had she known he would be riding a pony before she saw him on Jock? Maybe his mother had mentioned that to her.

Soon Gary's shirt was wet with sweat and the breeze felt good in the hot sunshine. As Gary mowed under the shade trees, he looked anxiously up into the limbs, trying to see if the old owl was there. Owls were supposed to sleep during the day, but that might be just another fairy tale, he decided. When no huge bird appeared, Gary decided this was his lucky day, for that old owl had sure scared him. He touched the scab on his cheek through the bandage. He didn't want to tangle with that creepy old owl again!

When Gary's mother drove in, she stopped near her son and waited for him to approach. "How are you doing, honey? Are you feeling okay?" she asked.

"Sure, Mom, I'm fine. Should I quit now?"

"No, not yet, Gary. We'll call you when lunch is ready and you can quit then. Mrs. Spoonaker said you only had to work mornings."

She drove on to the cottage and Gary resumed his mowing. Maybe he could make the ball game after all if he was free in the afternoon. He'd forgotten to ask what time of day the guys played in the schoolyard.

His daydreams ceased abruptly when the mower cut down a clump of wild flowers and bees swarmed angrily upward. At the first sight of the angry buzzers, Gary dropped the handle of the mower and ran toward the house, swinging his arms around his head to ward them off. If there was anything he really hated, it was getting stung by a bee. Some had stung him when he was little and as a result, to this day Gary hated bees and the honey they produced.

Now he ran as fast as he could toward the cottage. At the porch he raced up the steps two at a time and zoomed into the cottage. As he stood panting inside the closed door, Mrs. Spoonaker and his mother ceased their conversation and stared at him.

"What's the matter, Gary?" his mother asked.

"Bees," he gasped.

"Oh, dear," Mrs. Spoonaker said. "Mr. Kurlacher keeps hives for those pesky things and they're a nuisance to the whole county. Did you get stung, Gary?"

He shook his head, still trying to catch his breath.

"Bees, especially honeybees, go too far from their hives to feed," Mrs. Spoonaker continued, exasperation in her voice. "I have told Mr. Kurlacher they're a danger to children, but he makes his living selling honey so he doesn't listen."

"Mr. Kurlacher gave Gary the pony and saddle and even some boots," Mary said. "He seemed like a very kind man to me. As well as a generous one," she added.

"He is, he is," Mrs. Spoonaker answered, "but his bees are something else. Bee stings can be very dangerous, especially to anyone allergic to them. Bee stings can kill if enough occur at one time." She sighed. "However, Mr. Kurlacher has been bringing my groceries since my hip became too hurtful for me to go to town, so I don't complain about his bees very often. Since I have to stay indoors most of the time, I don't notice them when they come visiting."

By now Gary had caught his breath and he turned to go out the door.

"Let's have lunch," Mrs. Spoonaker said. "You have mowed enough grass today, Gary. Besides, it will take a while for those bees to move away and I don't want you to get stung."

"Let me fix lunch," Mary said rising. "You sit and rest that hip, Mrs. Spoonaker."

The old woman smiled. "I'll take you up on that, my dear, for I really don't enjoy the pain my hip gives me when I walk. Come, Gary, I'll introduce you to Beelzebub," she said, gesturing toward the big black cat sleeping on the hearth.

Gary sat down, but he eyed the cat dubiously, remembering the fury that had tried to attack him and Spike.

"Wake up, Bub," the old woman said.

The black cat opened one yellow eye and blinked at her as he flicked his tail.

"Beelzebub!" she said sternly. "Wake up and come here to me."

The cat opened his other eye as he sat up, then yawned and stretched. He carefully licked each front paw, then with a disdainful glance at his mistress and Gary, stalked out of the room toward the other part of the house.

Mrs. Spoonaker cackled, then said, "Cats do as they please, especially this one."

"That's a funny name," Gary said. "Bee-el...?"

"Beelzebub," Mrs. Spoonaker repeated. "I named him that because people said I was a witch and it seemed appropriate. I usually just call him Bub."

Gary was silent for a moment as he thought about

what she had said, then asked, "Are you really a witch?"

"Gary!" his mother said, shocked.

"No, no, it's all right," the old woman said. "I used to be a witch," she added, a twinkle in her eyes, "but nobody pays me to witch for them anymore, so I guess I am retired or perhaps just an over-the-hill witch."

"They *paid* you to be a witch?" Gary asked, eyes wide.

"Yes, they did," she answered. "When my husband was alive we made more money from my witching than we did from our farm. I witched wells for most of the people in this valley."

"How do you witch wells?"

She smiled at him, then answered, "I don't know where the expression 'witching wells' originated, but that's why people began calling me a witch. I could cut tree branches and when I walked around the area where a well was needed, when the branches turned toward the earth that was where water could be found."

"Golly," Gary said slowly.

"There really wasn't any witchcraft involved," she continued. "It has to do with body chemistry. When your body has the right chemical balance, then you can do it."

Gary considered the matter, then asked, "Then you can't really fly around on a broomstick, can you?"

The old woman cocked her head to one side and thought for a moment. "You know, Gary, I'm not really sure," she said slowly. "I have never tried it yet."

Gary returned her smile. "Then why does everybody call you a witch? Have you told them about your chemistry?"

She sighed. "Yes, I told them but it didn't do much good. People are frightened of things they cannot understand. When they tried using the same branches that I used, nothing happened, so they decided I was a real witch." She laughed, then continued, "Then when I found a baby owl about to die and raised him in my house until he could fly, that really touched off a storm. I freed the owl back into the wilderness, but he remembers and visits me. The story went around then that I had a familiar."

"What's that?"

"A familiar is a spirit creature who can get you in touch with the devil."

"Wow! Can you?" Gary asked. "Get in touch with the devil, I mean."

"Now why would anyone want to do that?" she asked, shaking her head. "I sure wouldn't, would you?"

"No, ma'am!"

"I named the black kitten I found Beelzebub just to tease everybody," she said. "You know that's another name for Satan, don't you?"

"No, ma'am, I didn't, but your cat really looked mean when he came after us."

"Which just shows you how dangerous it is to yell at a person and throw rocks at her house," Mary said, putting the last food on the table. "Come eat lunch now."

"How come you don't look for wells anymore?" Gary asked.

Mrs. Spoonaker sighed as she shook her head. "Geologists today can do the same thing with their instruments. Besides, I guess I'm too old and crippled to get around the way I once did. Nowadays I just grow herbs in that window you rascals broke, for herbs can do a lot of things today's medicines can't."

Gary glanced at the window that was now back in place, and he squirmed uncomfortably. "I said I was sorry," he muttered.

Then his mother and Mrs. Spoonaker changed the subject to other matters and Gary discovered he was hungry. He filled his plate and began to eat. How many Saturdays would it take, he wondered, before he had worked out his forty-dollar share of the damage? It wasn't that he minded pushing a mower. It was because bees could attack at any moment or a big old owl if he happened to be around. The old black cat didn't want to make friends, either, so he would have to leave Spike home when he came out here, at least until Bub and he got acquainted.

When the meal was finished, Mary rose. "While I clear up, Gary, why don't you put the mower away?"

"Should I mow anymore today, Mrs. Spoonaker?" he asked.

"No, you've mowed enough, Gary. Be careful the bees aren't around when you put the mower into the shed. If they're still buzzing around, just leave the old thing set where it is."

"I'll shoo them off if they're around," Gary said bravely, but in his heart he hoped they were gone.

Outside, only breeze filled the air. He walked slowly to where he had left the mower, looking in every direction for bees but they were gone. He pushed the mower to the shed and put it inside, then closed the door. When he returned to the front porch, his mother and Mrs. Spoonaker were emerging from the cottage.

"I'll see you next Saturday, Gary," Mrs. Spoonaker said. "Your mother said you could bring my groceries on your pony, so that will be a credit on your account."

"Yes, ma'am."

Gary went around to the barn corral and saddled Jock, then changed from sneakers to boots and climbed aboard. When he rode around the house, his mother's car was disappearing down the lane and Mrs. Spoonaker had gone back inside.

"Come on, Jock," he said. "Let's get going and maybe I'll make the ball game."

The pony pricked his ears, then went into a smooth canter that carried them swiftly over the ground.

CHAPTER SIX

A LOT OF BULL

ON SUNDAY MORNING Gary woke to the sound of rain and thunder and flashes of lightning. He could feel Spike shiver as he huddled as close to Gary as he could get. Absently, Gary patted his dog, saying, "Don't be afraid, Spike. The storm is just noisy."

Idly, Gary waited for a flash to show, then slowly counted one, two, three. Sure enough, the crack of thunder followed, just as his dad had told him. He could tell how many miles away lightning had struck by counting until the sound of thunder followed. Storms had frightened him when he was little until Dad had told him this. From then on he was too busy counting during a thunderstorm to be afraid anymore.

He squirmed into a more comfortable position and patted Spike again. "Maybe we won't have to go to church today, boy," he said. Church was okay, but wearing his suit was not. Somehow he was never

comfortable in his suit, but his mother always insisted he wear it to church.

Then his thoughts returned to yesterday and how different Mrs. Spoonaker had been from the things the guys said about her. She was okay to work for, he decided. He had gone over to the schoolyard as soon as he put Jock away, but nobody was there. The guys must have finished their ball game and left, so Gary returned home and helped with a few chores.

He rose, planning to ask his mother if they were going to church, when suddenly over the noise of the rain beating against the windows he heard a loud roar. When he looked outside he saw a big black bull butting his head against the shed, where Buttercup and her calf had taken refuge from the storm. Between hits the bull would raise his head and bellow his outrage and frustration.

Mary stuck her head in the door, saying, "I'm glad you're awake, honey. There's a bull trying to get to Buttercup and he'll break down anything in his way if we don't chase him away. Get dressed while I call the sheriff."

"It's a good thing he's an Angus without horns or he'd be doing more damage than he is," Gary said, then added, "Are we going to church?"

His mother glanced down at her good dress and made a wry face. "No, we aren't, and I had better change into something more practical before we go bull chasing."

Gary scrambled into his clothing from the day before. No use putting on clean clothing if he was going out into the rain. He knew cows came into breeding season shortly after calving, so that old bull must be answering Buttercup's smell. He wondered where the bull had come from, then decided Sheriff Thompson would probably know.

By the time he entered the kitchen his mother was on the phone telling the sheriff he was needed. Gary's stomach rumbled with emptiness but he decided breakfast would have to wait until the bull was chased away. He stuffed a cookie into his mouth and put another in his pocket for later. It might take awhile to get rid of the old bull.

"I'll go saddle Jock, Mom," he said as Mary hung up the receiver. "It'll be much easier than trying to chase him on foot."

"Oh, dear, what if that pony bucks again? Even if he has no horns, that bull's head is hard as granite and if he can get to you, he'll hurt you."

"Aw, Mom, Jock and I get along okay now. He'll be a big help to us."

"Well, okay," she said reluctantly, "but put on a raincoat and hat. Why is it always bad weather when stock acts up?" she added in an exasperated mutter.

Gary pulled on a slicker and jammed the raincap on his head. He was wearing sneakers instead of boots because he had a feeling he might have to run more than he would ride. Bulls were dangerous all the time, but especially when they wanted a cow. At least this one didn't have sharp horns to use on his rampage.

"You better stay inside here until the sheriff comes, Mom," he said. "It'll take a few minutes to get Jock saddled."

The sound of a thud against the shed, then the

crack of a board giving way against the attack, sounded through the noise of the rain.

"That bull isn't going to wait," his mother said. "I'm going to try to shoo him away." She was bundled into rain gear and had the broom in her hand.

Gary laughed, then asked, "Are you going to ride that or just beat up the bull with it?"

"Wish I could ride it," she muttered, then went out the door with Gary trailing behind her.

Gary saw his mother flourishing the broom at the big black animal as he went behind the shed and spied Jock using it for shelter of a sort. This time no oats were needed and Gary slipped the bridle over his pony's head and led him around to where the saddle was stored.

Mary was flailing away at the bull. He had his head lowered and was bellowing his frustration as he backed away from the swats Mary was landing on his head. Then he pawed angrily at the ground and Mary backed up against the shed.

"Hurry up, Gary," she urged. "I'm not making much of an impression with this broom."

Gary saddled the pony and had climbed up on him when Sheriff Thompson's car pulled into the driveway. He alit, came running to where Mary stood waving her broom, and took it from her.

"Go phone Kurlacher, Mrs. Benson," he said. "That's his Angus bull and he might just as well be helping us get him back where he belongs. Dang!" He squinted, then rubbed the water out of his eyes. "Wish this rain would stop!"

Gary silently echoed his wish for he could hardly

see in the downpour. The only one it didn't seem to bother was that old bull!

"Flank him on that pony, Gary, and we'll get him started for home. Kurlacher lives out just beyond Mrs. Spoonaker," the sheriff said.

The bull made a halfhearted charge at them, then stopped and pawed up slush with one huge hoof.

"Don't you dump me today, you old pony," Gary muttered to Jock. "Those feet are as big as my head and a lot harder." He urged Jock forward and the sheriff advanced with them, waving the broom as fast as he could.

The maneuver worked for just an instant as the bull backed away from his tormentors, but then the big black animal suddenly dodged around them and ran up to the shed again. Buttercup bawled and the bull tried again to butt his way into the shed. A board cracked as the hard head hit, but when he took a step backwards for another charge, Sheriff Thompson stepped into the void.

"Dang! Get back, you dumb brute," Sheriff Thompson said as he whacked the bull on the nose with the broom. "Get out of here! Come on, Gary, help me chase him home."

Gary dug his heels into Jock. "Come on, boy, let's herd cattle!" he said, then grinned to himself as he remembered watching cowboys who were always in some jam or other. Now he was really one of them! "Come on, Spike, help us get rid of this old pest!"

Spike had warily kept his distance from the raging animal but now he gave a tentative bark, then added his barks to the yells and noise going on.

With a lunge that almost unseated his rider, Jock

circled the bull to face him while the sheriff continued to swat the animal's nose as though he were swatting flies. When the bull lowered his head and pawed the ground, Jock snorted and did a little pawing himself. Spike barked furiously but kept his distance.

Gary took a firm hold on the horn of the saddle, then yelled, "Hee-yah! Get along little dogie! Hoo, haw, you old bull!"

Sheriff Thompson glanced his way, grinning even as he shook his head at the bedlam around him, then returned to flourishing the broom as the bull retreated from the shed. He paused to roar a protest into the downpour, but man and boy held their ground.

A pickup drove into the driveway and parked behind the sheriff's car. Mr. Kurlacher got out, swearing under his breath as the rain spattered him. He had his Sunday go-to-church suit on and swore again as the water teemed over him. Then he walked to where his bull was being held.

"Quiet, Spike," Gary ordered as the frantic barking grew louder. The dog looked a question at his master but ceased his barking.

"Thanks, Gary," the sheriff said wryly.

Mary emerged from the house but Sheriff Thompson waved her back. "You stay inside, Mrs. Benson," he called. "We'll take this critter home."

With Gary and Jock behind him and the two men flanking him, the bull apparently decided he was losing the battle. He snorted angrily as he walked in the direction he was driven. A flash of lightning filled the sky. Gary had only counted to two before the crack of thunder followed. That was pretty close! Jock trembled at the noise and Spike whimpered.

Gary touched his pony lightly in his flanks and they continued on their way. The bull roared back at the thunder but he, too, continued plodding on.

By the time the procession reached the Kurlacher farm, both men were covered with mud and Jock had mud splashed up to his belly. Spike's ears were dripping slop as he walked gingerly through puddle after puddle. He barked occasionally but kept himself beside the pony. Gary's sneakers were soaked and he was glad he hadn't worn his boots. The rain might have ruined them. Besides, he had discovered he could be a cowboy no matter what he wore.

"Hee-yah!" he yelled as they herded the bull into a strong corral. The huge hoofs splattered mud over his back as the bull came to an abrupt stop and whirled to face his tormentors.

"That will hold you," Mr. Kurlacher said, then angrily slammed the gate and barred it securely. "Come on in, sheriff," he said. "You, too, Gary. We better dry out some before we head back."

"Naw," Gary drawled in his best imitation of a cowhand. "We'll just mosey on back home. Why don't you phone my mother? She'll come get you in her car and you won't have to walk anymore." He squinted up into the sky. "Looks as though this rain won't stop anywhere soon."

"Sounds good to me," Sheriff Thompson said, then looked down at himself in dismay. "We better get rid of some of this mud so we don't foul up her car."

The two men disappeared into the house and after swiping the water off his face, Gary headed Jock homeward. Spike trotted along beside him and Gary decided he had never seen his dog this bedraggled. He fished the soggy cookie out of his pocket and broke it in half.

"Here, boy," he said as he leaned down to offer the piece of cookie. "We need to get home and dry out."

Spike gulped the morsel down and Gary stuffed the other half into his own mouth. He was ready for breakfast anytime!

Despite the miserable weather, Gary was feeling great. He and Jock had shown that old bull who was boss! Sure, the men had helped, but Gary bet the bull was more afraid of a man on a horse than anybody afoot.

When he neared home, his mother's car came along and stopped beside him. "Are you all right, Gary?" He nodded and she continued, "You are really soaked! When you get home climb into a hot bath before you put on clean clothing. I don't want you catching your death of cold."

"Will you let Spike ride, Mom? He's shivering."

Mary looked at the dripping dog and shook her head. "He would really mess up the car, honey. You're close enough to home. Get going and dry him out with you."

"Okay, Mom. Don't forget to get your broom back from the sheriff. We might need a ride some time." He grinned as he urged Jock onward and his mother pulled away. She had giggled at his words and it sounded good to him. Dad would want them to be happy if it was possible.

"Come on, cayuse," he drawled. "I have to take a hot bath and you have to let the rain wash off some of this mud." He flapped his heels against Jock. "Come on, Spike, let's get cracking." They completed the trip in a mud-splashing run.

While Spike rolled on some loose hay, Gary unsaddled Jock and took off the bridle, then turned him back into the pasture. When he inspected the shed where the bull had struck, one board was cracked but the building was still sound. Gary decided he would reinforce the board when it wasn't pouring rain.

"You okay, Buttercup?" he called.

There was no answer, but when he looked inside, Buttercup was contentedly chewing her cud while her calf slept beside her. Gary called to Spike and hurried to the house to do as his mother had ordered.

It felt good to rid himself of his soaked clothing. He decided he would eat breakfast before he soaked in any old tub. A guy had to have nourishment after what he had been through, didn't he?

Spike had rubbed much of the grime from his coat so the tracks he left on the kitchen floor weren't really too bad. Gary fed his dog first and then himself. When they had eaten, they headed for the bathroom to wash off the rest of the grime that was still on them. Gary boosted Spike into the tub and climbed in after him. He soaped his protesting dog liberally and rinsed him off under the tap.

"Hold still, boy," he said as Spike wriggled in his grasp. "Now sit while I get clean."

He repeated the soaping and rinsing on himself, then climbed dripping from the tub. Spike put his front feet on the edge and whined in protest.

Gary grabbed a big towel before he lifted Spike onto the mat beside the tub, then rubbed him as dry as he could. He used another towel to dry himself before he went racing to his room with his dog at his heels. While Spike rolled on the rug, Gary climbed into clean clothing.

By the time Mary returned and left the men beside their cars, the rain had stopped. She came into the kitchen carrying a quart jar of honey.

Gary grimaced as she set the jar on the table. "Why'd you buy that?" he asked. "I thought you didn't like honey either."

"I didn't buy it," his mother answered. "Mr. Kurlacher insisted I take it because of the trouble his bull caused. I couldn't refuse without being impolite."

"Oh."

She smiled at him. "I'll ask Mrs. Spoonaker if she can use it when she calls about her grocery list. If she can, you may take it to her on Saturday."

Gary nodded. He went to peer out a window and said, "It's too sloppy to go outside. Okay if I watch television?"

"I suppose so," she answered. "You did a full day's work this morning. If there isn't anything special on, how about reading for awhile? Didn't you start a book a while back that you haven't finished?"

He nodded. "It's about cowboying, too, so maybe I better get to it and see if there's anything I missed this morning."

"I saw you herding that animal and I think you did great," she said. "Jock, too," she added. "I don't think they would have gotten that bull back home so easily without you cowboying for them."

Gary smiled. When his mother praised him it always

gave him a great feeling. Then he decided to make her smile, too, as he asked, "Did you remember your broom?"

She laughed, then answered, "I left it in the car. I doubt if it will be much use as a broom again, but we can use it in the shed, I suppose. I'll buy another the next time I'm at the store." She glanced at the tracks on the floor. "I'm glad I didn't use the mop on that animal."

The phone rang and Mary went to answer it. Gary ambled into the living room and turned on the television, idly flicking from station to station.

When his mother came in, she was frowning.

"What's the matter, Mom?"

"I'm not sure," she said slowly. "That was Mrs. Allen calling. She said her son and John James and Willie Haus are all sick. Very sick. She wanted to know how you were feeling. When I told her you were fine, she said it was probably because you were working for the 'old witch'—Mrs. Spoonaker. It seems that only you and Billy Walker are well of the boys who deviled her the other night." She paused, thinking.

"What made them sick, Mom?"

She shook her head in exasperation. "Mrs. Allen said it was a spell cast on them by Mrs. Spoonaker. The doctor doesn't seem to know what it is or what to do about it."

"Gosh!" Gary exclaimed, eyes wide. "How come Billy wasn't included? She saw him as the leader."

Mary sighed. "I don't know, honey, and I certainly don't think Mrs. Spoonaker is a witch. She explained how they started calling her that, didn't she?"

"Maybe she was putting on a act to fool us, Mom," Gary said with a shiver. "Maybe she just doesn't want us to know she really is a witch."

They stared at each other, considering the matter.

CHAPTER SEVEN

BUTTERCUP'S BINGE

WHEN GARY ARRIVED at school on Monday morning, the place was in an uproar. Billy was talking a mile a minute about how the "old witch" should be arrested! Hadn't she cast a horrible spell over the boys who had annoyed her?

"How come you aren't sick?" Gary asked. "We were there, too, weren't we?"

"You're doing her work for her," Billy said with a sneer. "Just you wait—she'll get you yet!"

"How come you aren't sick?" Gary repeated.

"Me? Hah! I'm too strong for her to fool around with and she knows it!"

"Aw, you're just a kid like the rest of us," Gary said scornfully. "I don't think Mrs. Spoonaker is a witch, but if she is, my mother said she was too old to do anything like that. She can't even get into town anymore."

"Witches don't have to move around to do things," Billy insisted. "She's just getting even for us baiting her and breaking her old window."

"Did you guys pay your parts yet?" Gary asked.

"Naw, and we ain't gonna," Billy answered. "I told the guys to tell their parents to forget it. That old witch can't make us do anything, only Willie was scared. His folks paid his forty dollars. See what it got him? He's sicker'n a dog, just like Jimmy and John. Yesterday they were all pitching their cookies all over the place."

Miss Black came into the room and quieted the uproar. "Settle down now," she ordered. "Let's get on with our lessons." She glanced around at her pupils, then added, "If any of you feel ill, please let me know immediately. Dr. Haines has not yet determined what is wrong with the boys who are ill, but if it is something catching, class will be dismissed."

Billy stood up. "I feel sick, Miss Black. I think you should dismiss us before I get sicker."

She walked to where he stood and peered closely into his eyes and felt his forehead to see if he had a temperature. Billy moaned as though in agony, but he didn't fool her.

"Billy Walker, I don't think you are ill at all. Now sit down and let's get on with our work," she said, then turned and went to her desk in the front of the room.

When the school day ended, Gary left as quickly as he could to avoid Billy. Heather Johnson ran to catch up with him and her admiration showed in her eyes.

"Gary, what was she like? I mean the old witch. Did you work for her Saturday? Did her cat change back into a human?" she asked, her words tumbling over each other.

Two girls joined them and Gary found himself surrounded by curious females. Susan and Becky

Kohler were as interested in Mrs. Spoonaker as Heather, voicing their curiosity as question after question spilled from their mouths.

"Hey, wait up there," Gary said, quieting them. "Mrs. Spoonaker was real nice. Her cat stayed a cat, only he didn't want to be bothered, so he left. My mother and I ate lunch with her."

"You did?" Heather asked, her eyes widening in wonder. "You really ate something she had fixed?"

"My mother fixed lunch for all of us."

"Was her owl around?" Becky asked. "Did he bite you again?"

"He didn't bite me the first time," Gary said. "He scratched me with his talons while he was flogging my head. It didn't last long. He only comes to visit Mrs. Spoonaker once in a while and he wasn't around Saturday."

"She's a witch," Susan said stubbornly. "Everybody knows she's a witch. Just look what she did to Willie and the others. She's cast a spell on them and they might even die."

"Maybe they just got sick from something else," Gary said, then told them how Mrs. Spoonaker had witched wells. That was why people had started calling her a witch.

"She *is* a witch!" Susan insisted. "Nobody else could make her old sticks point to where there was water. I asked my mother and that's what she said, so there!"

"I have to go home," Gary said, edging away from them. "I have to do homework and chores. See you tomorrow."

He hurried on home, wondering how you could

convince people they were wrong about something when they were so sure they were right. Or was he the one who was wrong? Was Mrs. Spoonaker really a witch after all? Could she have been putting on an act for his mother and him? He shook his head in bewilderment.

When he arrived home there was a strange pickup in the driveway and he wondered who was visiting them. As he approached the house, he heard Spike whining inside when he usually came bounding to meet Gary. Inside, there was no sign of a visitor or his mother, so Gary sternly told Spike to "Sit!" before he went outside again and to the shed. In the lot behind, both his mother and a man were watching Buttercup. Jock had retreated to a far corner to graze, warily keeping one eye on his pasture mate who was usually so calm.

Gary stared as the cow staggered around, bawling as loud as she could, stumbling over a clump of flowers while her calf tried valiantly to stay beside her.

"What's wrong, Mom?"

Mary turned. "Oh, Gary, you're home," she said, then returned to watching the milk cow's antics. "This is Dr. Jacobs, Gary. I phoned him to come when I noticed Buttercup's strange behavior. Dr. Jacobs is a veterinarian. Doctor, this is my son, Gary."

Gary shook hands with him, then asked, "What's wrong with Buttercup?"

The cow bawled loudly, then suddenly fell on her side and kicked all four legs in a mad dance in the air. The doctor went to where she lay and began his examination.

"She acts as though she's drunk," he said, then

opened her mouth and sniffed at the odor that emerged. "By golly, I think she really is!" he exclaimed, making a face at the smell.

Buttercup dodged his hands and staggered to her feet. Then she lowered her head and pawed the ground like a bull, roaring as she threw up the dirt.

"Let's get out of here," Dr. Jacobs said, herding Gary and his mother before him. "Cows aren't like bulls when they charge. Bulls close their eyes and plow straight ahead but cows keep their eyes open and focused on whatever they are charging, so they are more dangerous. You folks get out of here before she horns you. Quick, now!"

"How could my cow be drunk?" Mary asked indignantly. "I never heard of such a thing."

They were outside the fence before Dr. Jacobs paused to look over the lot. His eyes stopped at a tree in a faraway corner of the pasture.

"What kind of tree is that?" he asked.

"I don't know," Mary said slowly. "We just recently moved here and I hadn't noticed it before."

He shook his head and strode around the fence to where the tree was located. Gary muttered, "Stay here, Mom," and followed him.

When they arrived at the tree, Dr. Jacobs sniffed the air. "I thought so!" he said. "This is an apple tree and those are rotten apples on the ground. Go get a sack, Gary, and we'll get rid of the rest of them before your fool cow eats any more."

"You mean *apples* made her drunk?" Gary asked incredulously.

"They more than likely fermented inside her stomach after she ate them," Dr. Jacobs answered. "I'll give her something to sober her up, but we had better get rid of the rest of them before she eats any more."

Gary ran back to tell his mother what Dr. Jacobs had said, then grabbed a feed sack and hurried back. Dr. Jacobs had climbed the fence into the pasture and motioned Gary to do the same. Jock stood in the opposite corner. He whinnied at Gary but he didn't come to meet him.

"Keep your eye on the old fool, Gary, and help me collect all these apples, rotten or otherwise," Dr. Jacobs said, stooping to gather some of the soft fruit into the sack. "You had better come out and collect the apples that fall every day so this doesn't happen again."

"How come Jock isn't drunk?"

"Ponies are smarter than cows," Dr. Jacobs answered.

Warily, Gary threw old apples into the sack while he kept an eye on Buttercup. She was staggering in circles and bawling her head off. Suddenly she paused, then vomited onto the ground.

"That's good," Dr. Jacobs said. "She'll get some of these out of her system that way and recover sooner."

They continued sacking apples, old rotten ones as well as the recently dropped apples. When Buttercup finished throwing up, she lay exhaustedly on the ground, her head still weaving from side to side.

Gary laughed. "That old gal sure had herself a binge. I saw an old drunk once when he was laying in the gutter and he looked as bad as she does."

"It's nothing to laugh about," the veterinarian said sternly. "Alcoholics are sick people who can't cope with the world, so they drink. Your cow will feel as bad as any alcoholic for a day or so, so feel sorry for her, not amused."

"Yes, sir," Gary answered, wiping the smile off his face.

When the apples had all been gathered, Gary dragged the sack behind him as they returned to the shed.

"I'll give your cow a shot, Mrs. Benson. It will help to sober her up, but those apples should be gathered every day as they fall so it doesn't happen again."

"I said I'd gather them, Mom," Gary said. "I'll go out after school and again in the morning before I leave and pick up the ones that have fallen."

Dr. Jacobs nodded. "That's the thing to do, son. Now, will you help me give the cow a shot? Can you hold her head down for me?"

"Yes, sir," Gary answered, then a thought struck him. "Do you suppose this is what's wrong with the guys at school? I heard they were throwing up, too."

"I haven't seen them, but I doubt very much if boys would eat rotten apples," Dr. Jacobs said wryly.

Gary went to Buttercup with the doctor and sat on the ground where he could get a hold on her head. Buttercup rolled her eyes at them and bawled, but feebly. She tried to get up when Dr. Jacobs jabbed a needle into her, but Gary tightened his grip on her head, careful to avoid the tips of her horns. They were too short to get a grip on, but they could probably do a lot of damage if she stuck them into a guy, he decided.

The vet rose. "Let's get out of here, Gary. We'll leave her alone now and let her get over her hangover. It's a good thing nobody has to milk her but her calf."

He walked to where he had left his bag beside

Mary and put the syringe away. "Your cow will be all right now, Mrs. Benson, but I had better look in on her tomorrow to be sure," he said.

"Thank you, Dr. Jacobs," Mary said. "Would you like me to pay you now?"

"I'll send a bill, Mrs. Benson, after I check your cow again tomorrow. Thanks for the help, Gary."

"Any time, Doc," Gary answered, then saw his mother frown.

"Don't be so flippant, Gary. This is Dr. Jacobs, not Doc," she said.

The doctor smiled and shook his head. "That's okay, son. Doc is what most people call me and I don't mind." He closed his bag, then tipped his hat to Mary before heading for his pickup.

Mary took another long look at her cow. Buttercup had lowered her head and was snoring loudly. Jock cautiously approached the sleeping animal, then sniffed at her and retreated back to the far corner of the pasture.

"She'll sleep it off, Mom," Gary said, trying to ease her mind. "She'll probably be as good as new tomorrow." Then curiously, "Are you going to have her bred again? Maybe we should have let that old bull do the job before we shooed him home."

Mary shook her head. "Buttercup is getting too old to have more calves. I thought we'd use her milk until she dries up again, then find a pasture where she can live out her life just grazing." She paused, then shook her head again. "We've had her since she was a calf and I wouldn't have the heart to let her be butchered."

"Is she older than me, Mom?"

"Is she older than *I*," his mother corrected. "No,

she isn't." She thought for a moment, then answered slowly, "You were about three years old when Buttercup was born so she must be at least seven years old. That's a lot of years for a cow, but she had always had good care and plenty of feed so she has stayed in good shape. She was never sick until today. My, it really gave me a turn when I saw her acting up as she did."

Gary laughed. "She sure looked spooky when she was pawing and bawling, didn't she? Going on a binge at her age!"

"I doubt she thinks it's funny," his mother said soberly. "Poor old darling, she must feel terrible."

Gary swallowed the quip on his tongue. This was no time to tease. Old Buttercup had been around as long as he could remember. She was a nice old cow that he had played around at milking time while his parents were working. Buttercup had become a family pet, which was why his mother hadn't sold her along with the rest of the livestock when they sold the farm. Instead, she had the cow trucked to their new home in Bellarosa.

As they walked to the house Gary grinned to himself. Who would think an old cow like that would get smashed on rotten apples? Maybe it wasn't funny to her, but Buttercup had sure cut some wild circles like no cow Gary had ever seen.

CHAPTER EIGHT

PONIES AND PAINT

O N TUESDAY WHEN Gary returned to school, the weather was calm. Clouds still lingered here and there but they were white and fleecy instead of gray and menacing. Bellarosa had been washed and drenched, puddles still lying in potholes in the road, but the houses and trees looked clean and shiny after the rain on Sunday.

In the schoolhouse yard the children were gathered into small groups. Low murmurs arose instead of the usual laughter and shrieks.

Gary looked around for somebody he could talk to, but then the bell rang and the students filed silently into the building. Gary caught up with Heather at the door.

"What's the matter with everybody?" he asked.

"More of the kids are sick," she answered, then faced him with tears in her eyes. "Your old witch is putting spells on the whole town, isn't she?"

Gary stared at her. "What are you talking about,

85

Heather?" he asked incredulously. "Mrs. Spoonaker isn't really a witch and she sure isn't 'mine' at any rate."

Heather tossed her head indignantly and left him.

"What the heck," Gary muttered, then followed her into the classroom.

Miss Black called the class to order, then looked around at her students. "Some more children have been taken ill," she said. "Dr. Haines has not yet determined just what the illness is, but some adults are also sick. Whatever it is, it isn't confined to this school so we'll just proceed as usual."

"It's the old witch," Billy Walker said loudly. "She's making everybody sick just because she's mad."

"Be quiet, Billy," Miss Black said. "You must not accuse people of anything if you don't have proof."

Gary raised his hand.

"What is it, Gary?" she asked.

"Mrs. Spoonaker wouldn't hurt anyone," he said with a defiant look at Billy. "She's a nice old woman, that's all."

"Ha!" Billy sneered. "She probably put a spell on you just so you'd think that. She only wants you to do her work for her."

"My mother ate lunch with her and she thinks Mrs. Spoonaker isn't a witch, at least not one that would put spells on people," Gary insisted.

"That's enough now," Miss Black said. "It is time we did some work in here."

It wasn't until the next day that the schoolhouse really buzzed with curiosity. Willie Haus walked in, pale and smiling sheepishly, but ready to get to his lessons.

"It is certainly nice to see you back, Willie," Miss Black said. "Are you well?"

"Yes'm," Willie answered. "Ma gave Mrs. Spoonaker the forty dollars for my part of her broken window and she lifted the spell."

"What'd I tell you?" Billy said with a sneer. "That old bat just wants her money."

Miss Black ignored Billy's outburst. "Did Dr. Haines say you were fit to come to class, Willie?"

"Yes'm."

"Did he say what had made you ill?"

"No'm. He just checked me over and said he couldn't find anything wrong with me, but I sure was sick for a few days," he said, making a face.

The wail of a siren sounded in the distance, preceding the entrance of the principal. Mr. Dickens greeted Miss Black, then turned to the class.

"Glad to see you have recovered, Willie," he said soberly. "I'm afraid Jimmy Allen and his mother haven't fared so well. An ambulance came from the hospital to take them both where they have better facilities. Jimmy became ill first and Dr. Haines is afraid he might die from the severe convulsions he has been having."

"Oh, dear, that's awful!" Miss Black said, shaking her head and frowning.

"Yes, it is," Mr. Dickens agreed.

"Perhaps at the hospital they can determine just what causes the illness," Miss Black said soberly.

"It's a witch's spell!" Billy said defiantly.

"That's enough of that kind of talk, Billy," the

principal said. "There is a reasonable explanation for everything and I am sure there will be one for this."

Billy subsided into his seat, muttering under his breath. Gary bit his lip to keep himself quiet. There was no use trying to convince Billy of anything.

The rest of the week was bewildering. Some of the children who had been taken sick returned to class, but some remained home in bed, still with varying symptoms. Other adults were ill. Some recovered in just a day or two while others remained miserably sick. It was a mystery Dr. Haines could not unravel. He dosed and tried different medicines, but the cause of the epidemic eluded him. He went to the hospital where Jimmy and his mother lay, but their illness was still a puzzle. Jimmy, especially, steadily grew worse.

On Saturday Gary saddled Jock and rode to Mrs. Spoonaker's house to do chores. He carried her groceries in a bag behind the saddle. The quart of honey was inside, for the old woman had told Gary's mother she would love to have some honey for herself.

After Gary unloaded the groceries and carried them inside, Mrs. Spoonaker thanked him, then said, "Will you paint on that old barn and corral out back, Gary? There's white paint in the shed. The corral, especially, certainly could stand some freshening."

"Sure," Gary answered. "I did a lot of fence painting while we still had our farm."

He got a gallon of white paint from the shed and pried it open with a screwdriver, then took the paint and a big brush he found to the corral where he had left Jock. Jock came to the fence to sniff the paint, then snorted and retreated to the other side.

"It doesn't smell so good, hey, boy?" Gary wrinkled his nose at the odor, then dipped the brush in the can and began to smear the paint on the old boards.

Weather had destroyed most of the former coat of paint, but there were still patches of it clinging to the boards. Gary knocked off the pieces that were loose, covered the ones that were still tight, and admired his work as the surface became solid white under his brush. When he grew tired of stooping to dip his brush into the paint, he perched the can on one of the railroad ties that had been used as posts. His back felt better when he remained erect.

The sun rose higher as Gary slapped paint on the sections of corral, moving his can of paint from post to post as he progressed. Jock came over to stick his nose between the boards, begging for the sugar cubes Gary often gave him.

"Get away, you old beggar," Gary said, slapping the pony's nose with his free hand. "I didn't bring any sugar for you today."

Jock snorted angrily, tossing his head as he raced around the corral. Then he returned to where Gary worked and again stuck his nose through the crack.

"Get back, Jock," Gary said, then used the brush to wipe some paint on the soft nose. He laughed at the sight.

Jock jerked back and shook his head, but the paint smear stayed where it was. Then he tossed his head and tipped the can of paint over Gary, whinnying at the results.

With a yell, Gary dropped the brush and wiped the

paint out of his eyes. The white coating covered his head and shoulders and dripped down onto his clothing and shoes. He stared at the mess, then raced to the water tank to try to wash it off.

He dipped his head into the water and scrubbed at his hair with both hands, then did the same for his face. His hair felt stiff when he raised it and shook off the water. He swiped at it with a shirt sleeve and only succeeded in smearing more paint over himself.

"Darn you, Jock," he said angrily. "My clothes are ruined and I'll probably lose my hair and it's all your fault. *Now* what should I do?" He gazed despairingly at his paint-smeared shirt and jeans.

Mrs. Spoonaker must have looked out a kitchen window for she raised it and called, "Gary! Come here and we'll see if we can clean you up. My, what a mess!"

"Yes'm."

Gary picked up the can, noting that most of the paint that had not covered him had spilled onto the ground. He put the cap on the can and pounded it into place, then returned to the shed and located some brush cleaner. After slushing the brush through the contents, he eyed the cleaner thoughtfully. Would it take the paint off of him, too?

Mrs. Spoonaker called to him from the front porch and Gary went to meet her.

"Oh, dear," she said, "you have ruined your clothing!"

"Would brush cleaner take off the paint?" he asked.

She shook her head. "It would probably take off your clothing and skin, too," she answered. "I'm afraid it's too strong to use on yourself."

Gary looked down at himself and sighed.

"You had better get yourself home, Gary," the old woman said. "Your mother will probably know how to clean you up. I was going to give you lunch, but the quicker you get those clothes to your mother, the better it will be. Once paint really sets it's as hard as iron."

"I'm sorry I spilled your paint," Gary said.

"I saw that pony dump it on you," Mrs. Spoonaker said indignantly. "I think he did it on purpose!"

Gary grinned as he shook his head. "I put paint on him first, so it was my fault, I guess."

"Well, go saddle the rascal up and make him take you home as fast as he can," she said. "I'll see you next Saturday and there is more paint in the shed."

"Yes, ma'am," Gary said, then went and saddled Jock, scolding at him all the time.

When Jock slowed down on the ride home, Gary nudged him in the ribs with his sneakers. It was a good thing he hadn't worn his boots, he decided. The white mess had even splattered his high-tops.

"Get along, you old cayuse," he said in his best cowboy imitation. "Think you're smart, don't you?"

A flick of ears and tail was his only answer.

When Gary reached home he unsaddled Jock and put him and the tack away. Buttercup grazed peacefully in the lot, her calf at her side. You would never have known she was the same animal who had eaten too many rotten apples. Gary shook his head as he watched her. Now *he* was in trouble. Maybe trouble just ran in the family.

Mary stared when he came in the house and stood before her. "What happened?" she asked, aghast.

"Aw, Jock knocked a bucket of paint off the post and

I was under it, Mom. Mrs. Spoonaker sent me home so the paint wouldn't harden before you could get it off."

"Your hair!" his mother wailed. "You have paint in your hair!"

"I know," Gary said, making a face. "I wanted to try brush cleaner on it but Mrs. Spoonaker said it would take skin and all off with the paint. She said you'd know what to do. Do you?" he asked hopefully.

"I don't know," she said uncertainly. "Go put other clothing on and I'll try." She groaned, then added, "What next?"

Gary hurried up the stairs and carefully piled the paint-smeared shirt and jeans so no paint would touch the chair, then dressed himself and took the bundle back to his mother.

She took it from him and placed the clothing in the washing machine. "I'll try bleach on these and see what happens. It's a good thing they're fairly old. If the paint doesn't come out there will be little lost."

"What about my hair, Mom?"

Mary finished pouring bleach and soap into the machine, then closed the lid and turned it on. Then she turned to look at Gary.

"Come over by the sink, honey. I'll try soap first and if that doesn't work, maybe a little bleach will do the job." She put a towel around his shoulders, then waited until he hung his head over the sink.

After letting warm water run over Gary's hair, Mary lathered his head and scrubbed his hair as hard as she could. When she rinsed away the soap, however, the paint still showed in ghastly streaks on his head.

"Well now, I'll try some bleach," she said grimly.

Gary grunted, head still hung over the sink.

His mother mixed bleach in a cup of water, then sloshed it over her son's head. She rubbed and rubbed until finally the paint began to soften and rinse away when she turned the water on Gary's hair.

"I think that does it!" she said triumphantly. "Stay put while I use another cup to get rid of the rest of the paint."

Gary stayed patiently in place while she mixed another cup of bleach and water, then poured it onto his hair and again rubbed away.

When his mother had again rinsed Gary's hair, she squeezed the water from it and wrapped his head in a towel. Then as she vigorously toweled his hair dry, he straightened, hoping the paint was all gone. When his mother removed the towel, she stared for a moment, then began to giggle helplessly.

With a baffled look, Gary walked to the mirror in the living room to see how he looked. The boy who looked back at him had yellowish streaks in his otherwise brown hair and Gary's heart sank.

"Mom!" he wailed, running into the kitchen. "I can't go anywhere looking like this! Oh, Mom, it's terrible!"

Mary sobered as she nodded. "It will grow out, honey. At least the paint is gone."

"Mom-m-m," he said mournfully. "Do something! Please?"

"Calm down, Gary. I'll go get some rinse the color of your hair. I think it will cover the streaks."

While she was gone Gary roamed restlessly from room to room. Wouldn't the guys hoot if he showed up with bleached streaks in his hair? They would never let him live it down!

When Mary returned from town with a bottle of color rinse, her face had a worried look. She handed Gary the bottle without a word and he went to the sink again and drenched his hair with the contents. After he had thoroughly rubbed the liquid in and then dried it, he went to the mirror to inspect the job. It was better! All the streaks had been covered. Then he returned to the kitchen.

"Look, Mom, it worked!" he said happily, then noticed her stricken face. "What's the matter?"

Mary sighed. "I guess I might as well tell you," she said. "You'll find out anyway. Jimmy Allen is dead. He died in the hospital this morning."

Gary stared at her. Jimmy was even younger than his father had been. How could he have died? A shiver ran over his shoulders. His mother had explained death to him when his father died, but he still didn't understand just *why* it had to happen.

"Are you okay, honey?" his mother asked as Gary stood mute. "Your friend is dead and I know how badly you feel, but there is nothing anyone can do to bring him back. He's in God's hands now."

"Why, Mom? Why do people have to die?"

Mary shook her head. "Only God can answer that question, Gary. Life and death are His decisions." Then her eyes filled with tears as she said, "I wish I had an answer for myself, but I don't. We just have to accept." She held out her arms and Gary moved into her comfortable embrace.

They clung to each other for a time until Mary held Gary away so she could see his face. "You and I have seen too much of death lately, honey, but we can take it, can't we?"

Gary blinked at the tears in his eyes as he nodded. His mother handed him her handkerchief and he blew vigorously before handing it back to her. "Guess we can take anything, can't we, Mom?" Then a thought came to him. "Will I die soon, Mom?"

"Of course not!" she exploded. "I started squirting vitamins down your throat when you were just a baby, remember? And remember all those inoculations the doctor gave you? You would always start to yell when I pulled into his parking lot, and you kept it up until we drove away!"

A reluctant smile twitched Gary's lips. "Guess I just didn't like to be stuck, Mom. Guess I was a real pain in the neck."

"Oh, no. You were our precious son and your father and I did everything we could to keep you healthy. You'll probably live to be a hundred."

"With a long beard," Gary added, then said soberly, "I wish Jimmy hadn't died, don't you?"

"Of course, honey. Jimmy was just a boy." She paused, thinking, then said, "The terrible part of all this is that people are blaming Mrs. Spoonaker."

Gary stared, bewildered, then said, "She wasn't anywhere near Jimmy, Mom. I was out there with her all morning."

"I know, honey, but some of these people are very superstitious. They think she's a witch and is casting spells over the people who have become sick. Now that Jimmy Allen is dead, there is no telling to what lengths they will go."

"You mean they might hurt her?"

Mary nodded. "They might try if Sheriff Thompson can't calm them down. Some people in the store were talking about her and they said she is a murderess!"

CHAPTER NINE

HOW GOOD IS GOOD?

WHEN SUNDAY ROLLED around, Gary knew there was no escape. The sky was clear, there were no loud roars outside, and even Spike sat up and looked at him expectantly.

"Okay, boy, let's go," Gary said with a sigh. He went down the stairs with his dog beside him to let Spike outside.

Sure enough, Gary's mother was in the kitchen fixing breakfast and she was dressed in her best dress, so he knew they were going to church. A bib apron protected her.

"Morning, Mom."

She smiled at him. "Come eat breakfast before you get dressed, honey. Suits are harder to clean than pajamas," she said.

He slid into a chair at the table, then made a face. "Okay if I brush my teeth first?"

"I thought you had," she answered. "Sure, go ahead. The bacon isn't quite ready anyhow."

Gary rose and ran up the stairs to the bathroom. His mother had always told him to brush the sleep off his teeth before he ate. Things tasted better.

When he returned Spike was back in the kitchen in his favorite spot beneath the table. A plate of bacon and eggs was waiting for him, but now Gary was not so hungry. He had remembered Jimmy Allen was dead, now that he was fully awake. Somehow it had dulled his appetite.

"Don't look so sad, honey," his mother said. "Losing a friend is hard, I know, but life goes on."

"I was thinking about Mrs. Spoonaker mostly," he admitted. "She's been really nice to me...." He paused, then continued, "You don't think anyone will really believe she was the cause, do you?"

Mary sighed. "I just wish people weren't so superstitious," she said. "I've kidded with you about her being a witch, but I don't think she is one."

"I don't either," Gary said soberly, "but when I tried to tell that to Billy Walker, he wouldn't listen. He sure has a big mouth," he added.

"The most ignorant usually do," Mary said.

Gary nodded, then said, "It's funny, though, that Willie got well after his folks paid his share of the broken window, isn't it?"

"That was just coincidence, but it does make things look worse," she answered. Then she glanced at the clock. "Eat your food, honey. It's time we went and you still have to dress."

Spike nudged Gary under the table until a piece of bacon appeared.

"Pretty expensive dog food," his mother observed.

"Aw, Spike is worth it, Mom. He's a guard dog and

guards need their strength." He stuffed the last of the egg and toast into his mouth, then raced Spike up the stairs to his room.

After he was dressed in his Sunday suit and a white shirt, he paused in the bathroom to look at himself. "Just like a stuffed shirt," he muttered, then went to meet his mother.

Most of the congregation was inside when they arrived at the church, with only a few stragglers hurrying in. Preacher Lloyd Gray had just entered the pulpit and was opening the big Bible to the theme for his sermon. He glanced around at his flock, cleared his throat, then began to speak.

Gary listened for a minute or two, then his thoughts drifted away. Sermons always made him sleepy. He had decided some time ago it was better to keep himself awake with thoughts of his own than to fall asleep during church services. He thought about Jimmy Allen and the strange sickness that was affecting so many people. Why couldn't Dr. Haines determine what it was? There were so many different ways the sickness took. Some people were only sick to their stomachs for a few days, others had violent convulsions. One died. So far.

Then a thought occurred to Gary. Maybe Mrs. Spoonaker could help. The day his mother had eaten lunch with them, the old woman had explained how herbs could cure many ills. Before doctors had as much medicine they had relied heavily on herbs to cure different ailments. If the old woman could come up with a cure for whatever this was, then maybe people wouldn't accuse her of being a witch.

He glanced at his mother. After church he would

ask her if he could ride Jock. He didn't have to say he was going out to Mrs. Spoonaker's house, did he? His mother might think he was being a bother, but so long as she didn't tell him not to go, he could go, couldn't he? He puzzled over this for a moment, then nodded to himself. Just not saying something wasn't the same as a lie. Having made up his mind and feeling very virtuous, he made himself listen to the end of the sermon.

Preacher Gray was talking about the inevitableness of death and how children should be cherished as God's most wonderful gift. He also said that God called only the good to reside in His kingdom, and Gary retreated into his own thoughts again. Maybe he shouldn't be *too* good. He didn't want to be called anytime soon!

Mary nudged him to attention and Gary sat straighter.

"One of our flock has fallen to illness and died," Preacher Gray said. "Jimmy Allen's funeral will be held at ten tomorrow morning here in the church, then at the Bellarosa Cemetery. I hope you will all be there." Then he turned and walked away from the altar.

The silence in the church lasted for only a moment, then voices rose here and there as people drifted into groups and discussed the coming funeral.

Billy Walker's father could be heard over the hubbub as he said, "I think Sheriff Thompson should have arrested old lady Spoonaker before now!"

Gary sighed. He was just like his son!

Then Mr. Kurlacher spoke up. "Walker, what evidence do you have that Mrs. Spoonaker has anything to do with this? Your son was the ringleader of the broken window expedition and he hasn't been taken ill."

"That's because I paid the forty dollars that Ben said was Billy's share of the damage," Mr. Walker said angrily. "It's extortion, that's what it is! And now it's murder!"

Voices rose in a babble and arguments started both pro and con Mrs. Spoonaker. Tempers grew hot as differences were expressed, then Preacher Gray returned and rapped again for the attention of his flock.

"Quiet, please, ladies and gentlemen," he said. "We must not jump to conclusions. Mrs. Spoonaker is a member of this congregation even though she has been unable to attend services for some time now."

"She's a witch!" Billy shouted. His father nodded his approval.

"It has never been proved that Mrs. Spoonaker is anything other than a Christian woman who once did fine things for this community," Preacher Gray said. "When she and her husband first came to Bellarosa they were the only ones around who could find water where a well should be located."

"Doesn't that prove she's a witch?" Mr. Walker asked.

Gary stood away from his mother. "No, it doesn't," he said stoutly. "Mrs. Spoonaker said it was the . . . the chemistry in her body that made sticks point to where there was water."

"Aw, she's got him under a spell, too," Billy said scornfully. "He's been doing her chores and she's got him fooled along with his mother."

"I don't believe she's a witch, either, Billy," Mary said calmly, "so you are quite right about that. Mrs. Spoonaker is a lonely woman and more of us should visit her when we can. I doubt she has ever harmed a soul."

"Then you're as dumb as Gary," Billy said defiantly.

"Mind your manners, Billy," his father said sharply. "I am sorry, Mrs. Benson. My son should not have spoken to you as he did, but we feel very strongly that Mrs. Spoonaker is a very dangerous element in our community."

"That is purely superstition, Mr. Walker," Mary said. "I thought we were living in a more enlightened age."

"We aren't so enlightened that Dr. Haines can determine what is making our citizens ill or why Jimmy Allen died," Mr. Walker retorted.

"Our cow got sick from eating rotten apples that made her throw up," Gary said. "Maybe something like that is making people sick."

"Humph," Mr. Walker said scornfully. He turned to Dr. Haines, who up until now had remained quiet. "Well, Joe, could it be something that was eaten?"

Dr. Haines considered the question before he answered. "It might be," he said slowly. "The hospital has sent some specimens to the big laboratory in St. Louis for analysis. When we hear from them we might know more about the cause of all this. Until then, I just can't say."

Over the babble of voices that arose Preacher Gray again called for quiet. "Why don't you all go home," he said, "and return tomorrow for services for Jimmy Allen and his funeral. Meantime, let us all stay calm and not toss accusations around. Remember, we are Christians!"

Slowly, the groups of people dissolved as they left the church for their walk home or to get in a car and drive away.

"Let's go, Mom," Gary said urgently. "Let's go home. I'm hungry."

He wasn't especially hungry, but the sooner they ate lunch the sooner he could saddle Jock and go to see Mrs. Spoonaker. He didn't trust Billy or his father. What if they decided to go hurt the old woman some way? If he could talk to her first, at least she would have been warned. Maybe her herbs could help some of the people who were sick and then they wouldn't be so mad.

After he gulped his lunch, he asked, "Okay if I go for a ride on Jock, Mom? It's a nice day and some exercise would do him good."

"Go ahead," his mother answered. "You can use a little exercise yourself. You and I are becoming couch potatoes since...since your father passed away. It's time we both got out and around more than we do."

Gary nodded. "Spike needs exercise, too, so I'll take him with me. Come on, boy." He hoped the old owl and the black cat weren't around. He would leave Spike with Jock while he talked to Mrs. Spoonaker. If the cat were curled up on the hearth again, he wouldn't even know Spike was outside.

This time he put his cowboy boots on before he went to saddle Jock. He wouldn't have to push a lawn mower today so he could be a real cowboy. He tightened the cinch on the saddle and slipped on a bridle, then climbed aboard the pony.

Spike danced on his hind legs as Jock set off in a trot. When Spike barked, Jock snorted and began to gallop.

"Take it easy, Jock," Gary said. "You, too, Spike. You guys have to be friends." He slowed Jock to a walk and with Spike trotting alongside, the three headed for Mrs. Spoonaker's farm.

Gary looked at his dog and grinned to himself. A lot of cowboys had dogs, didn't they? Or was that sheepherders? Whatever, he liked having Spike near when he was having fun. The sun was shining brightly and he should be feeling good, but deep inside was the nagging worry of Jimmy's death and how a lot of people thought Mrs. Spoonaker was to blame. He shook his head. Today he would ask her and tell her what people were saying. Mom thought questions were rude, but since she wasn't along today maybe being rude was the best thing to do.

When he reached the road to Mrs. Spoonaker's house, he rode Jock to the porch and dismounted. He wouldn't be here long enough to have to put his pony in the corral.

"Stay, Spike," he ordered.

When he turned around to climb the steps, he was confronted with the black fury he had seen the night they baited the old woman. The cat must have been dozing on the porch before Gary arrived, but he wasn't sleeping now. His black fur was standing on end and his yellow eyes gleamed as he spit a challenge at Spike.

Spike answered with a growl of anger as he bared

his teeth at the fiery fury. "Sit, Spike!" Gary yelled, but he was too late. With a snarl of rage, Spike leaped to meet the black cat halfway. Before Gary could grab his dog, cat and dog were rolling on the ground in a growling, spitting frenzy. Yowls and the gnashing of teeth emerged from the tangle. Try as he might, Gary could not get a secure hold on Spike to pull him from the melee.

Then the door opened and Mrs. Spoonaker came out with her broom in hand. "Here, you devils," she said as she whacked away with her weapon. "Stop it! Do you hear me? Stop it this minute! Beelzebub, come here! Call your dog, Gary."

Gary shouted over the din, "Spike, come here! Come here, boy!" but the two combatants were too enraged to hear.

Then Spike got clear for a moment and Gary grabbed him. Beelzebub came clawing and spitting, but Mrs. Spoonaker used her broom and he crouched on the ground. Painfully, Mrs. Spoonaker hobbled down the steps, still flailing her broom. She picked up the black cat as she laid the broom aside, then quieted him.

"Well!" she exclaimed, puffing from her exertions. "It would seem you and your dog have come to call, Gary. Beelzebub has no manners to speak of, so you must forgive him. If you'll leave your dog out here with your pony, we'll go in and have tea." She paused, noticing bloody scratches on Gary's hand. "I have some disinfectant for that," she added.

Gary waited until she and Beelzebub were safely inside before he loosened his hold on Spike. Spike's nose was bleeding and he blinked one eye that had been scratched, then licked a paw that had been mauled. Gary looked despairingly at his bleeding hands and his mangled dog. Now he would have to tell his mother where he had been. He was in trouble again!

CHAPTER TEN

MAD HONEY

WHEN BEELZEBUB WAS safely inside the cottage, Gary let go his hold on Spike. "Stay," he ordered. When Spike obediently sat down close to Jock and began to lick his wounds, Gary climbed the steps and knocked on Mrs. Spoonaker's door.

"Come in," she said in her quavery voice. "Come in, Gary."

He opened the door and peeked inside. Beelzebub was again curled up on the hearth, his eyes closed and his hair no longer standing on end.

"It's safe," she said. "He's a lazy old cat who likes to sleep more than anything. Come over here and I'll disinfect those scratches."

Reluctantly, Gary crossed to the counter where she stood. To him disinfectant meant stinging smarts that usually brought tears to his eyes. He held out his bleeding hands and closed his eyes. Maybe this time he could squeeze back any tears that appeared.

"Well now, Gary," the old woman said, and there was amusement in her voice. "Open your eyes."

When Gary opened his eyes and looked up at her he could see she was smiling. Then he looked at his hands. Her touch must have been light as a fairy's, for he hadn't felt it when she bathed away the oozing blood. The scratches no longer bled!

"I thought it would sting," he said.

"Some disinfectants do," she said, gathering the bottles she had used and stoppering them. "This is made from herbs, not chemicals, so it does its job quietly."

"Thank you," Gary said.

She nodded. "Of course I'm glad to see you, but was there any special reason why you came visiting today?"

"Yes'm, there is, only..."

"Only what?"

"Well, a lot of people around here have been taken ill lately and Jimmy Allen died yesterday," he said slowly.

Again she nodded. "I heard about it."

"Well...did you hear that some people think you cast a spell to make them sick?"

She sighed, then said, "Whenever something bad happens around here, I usually get the blame. I've tried to explain to these ignoramuses that witching wells doesn't mean I'm a witch, but they prefer not to believe me."

"Some of them want to hurt you," Gary blurted out. "I thought I better warn you."

She studied his face for a moment, then put her hand on his shoulder. "You're a good boy, Gary, and I thank you. I think I have discovered the cause of all the sickness in this instance. I tried to phone Dr. Haines but there was no answer."

"You *have*?" he asked, wide-eyed. "Are you a witch?"

"Oh, dear, why is it that I have to be a witch to be smart? I'm an herbalist, Gary. Why do you think I'm a witch?"

"Well... you said you'd give me a ride on your broomstick, didn't you?"

"I was only teasing," she said. "I get impatient with all the talk about my being a witch and make jokes that I should not." She sighed, then added, "Perhaps if I solve the dilemma even the doctors are in, my standing in the community will be improved."

Gary smiled at her, feeling better. After all the teasing he had done in his life, he should have recognized it when it came from someone else.

"I'm glad you and your mother don't care for honey," she continued. "When I opened the jar you brought me, it didn't smell just right, but it took me a while to decide what was wrong." She patted a large volume on the counter. "This is my herbalist bible. It contains knowledge people knew long ago but have forgotten these days. Mr. Kurlacher has been selling his honey all over town and I think it is what's making people ill. His bees must have gotten nectar from some rhododendrons or laurel. The honey still tastes good, but it can be lethal."

"You mean *honey* killed Jimmy?" Gary asked.

"Yes, I think honey killed your little friend, although this type of poison usually doesn't go that far. I had better try to phone Dr. Haines again. He will know who is sick and who isn't and can spread the word about the honey," she said, dialing as she spoke.

"Dr. Haines?" she asked as her call was answered. "This is Mrs. Spoonaker. I have been trying to reach you because I think I have found what is causing the current rash of illness in this area."

She waited as the doctor spoke to her, then continued. "Kurlacher's honey has been contaminated with poisonous plants of some variety, probably rhododendrons or laurel. If you check your patients, you'll find they have been eating the honey."

Again a wait ensued as she listened. Gary watched, almost holding his breath so he wouldn't miss a word. He wanted to tell his mother just what she said, then let her help spread the news so people would let the old woman alone.

"The nectar caused a central nervous system poisoning. Do your patients have weakness and vomiting, mental confusion and even intoxication?" she continued, then waited for the doctor to answer.

She nodded, saying, "Yes, I think it is the honey. I have been trying to phone Mr. Kurlacher but there's no answer. Will you get word to the storekeeper to stop selling it?" She listened for a few moments, then said, "You're welcome, Dr. Haines. If you wish, I can fix up some herbal tonic that I think will ease some of the symptoms."

She waited again, then said, "Yes, I'll have it for you this evening when you come by. Goodbye, doctor."

The sound of cars squealing to a stop and loud voices accompanied by Spike's barking took Gary to the window to see what was happening. Two cars full of men were outside the house and they were emerging from the cars, still with angry shouts filling the air. Gary hurriedly locked the door, then returned to the window.

"Get out here, you old witch," Billy's father yelled. "Come on, men, let's hang her to the highest tree!"

Gary turned from the window. "There are men with guns out there, Mrs. Spoonaker. Let's slip out the back door and hide in the woods."

A banging on the front door brought Gary's eyes to it. He was glad it was locked. Then he heard a yip from Spike as a boot connected with his ribs, and Gary's fists closed.

"I can't walk fast enough, Gary," Mrs. Spoonaker said, shaking her head. "If I call Sheriff Thompson perhaps he can get here quick enough to stop whatever is planned."

Just then a shoulder hit the front door and a voice roared, "Open the door, you old hag!" Other voices joined the first and a shadowy form showed outside the window as someone tried to see through the curtains.

"You in there, witch?" Billy's father asked angrily. "We'll get you anyhow, so you'd better open up!"

Gary thought fast, then asked, "Is there any place here in the house where you can hide so they can't find you?"

"Can you move that table and the rug under it?" Mrs. Spoonaker asked in a whisper. "There is a trapdoor to an old cellar that nobody knows about. If I can get down there and if you can replace the rug and table, I doubt anyone will think to look for a place such as that."

She wheezed as she hobbled around trying to help

Gary move the table, but since it was made of light pine wood, he moved it quite easily. She paused to catch her breath as Gary set the chairs aside and rolled up the throw rug. The faint outline of a trapdoor appeared.

"How does it open?" Gary whispered, although the noise from the porch was growing in volume.

"Push a little on this side."

Gary looked puzzled, but put his weight where she had ordered. The other side of the trapdoor opened enough for him to get a hand beneath it, and he pulled the weighted door open wide. Below were steps leading into total darkness.

The front door cracked and groaned as bodies slammed against it again and again.

"Hurry!" Gary whispered. He held one of her arms as the old woman laboriously made her way down the steps into the darkness below. Just before she disappeared into the dark cellar she turned and looked up at Gary.

"Will you be all right, Gary? They won't hurt you, will they?"

"No'm. You just be quiet," he said, motioning her to go down. With a worried look, she merged with the inky black of the hole in the ground.

Quickly, Gary let the trapdoor close, then hurried to put the rug in place. He grunted as he lifted the table and put it on the rug, then the chairs around the table.

The frenzy outside was growing and he knew the solid old door could not stand much more. He looked around, then as a finishing touch added some plates and cups on the table, grabbed a cookie from the jar, and bit it in half before placing the remains on a plate.

Rubbing his eyes, he went to the front door and unlocked it, then pulled it open. Spike came from behind and shot inside to be with Gary.

"Whadda ya want?" Gary asked, yawning as he knuckled one eye.

"What are you doing here?" Billy's father asked. "Where is old Mama Spoonaker?"

There was a chorus of echoes as other men pushed in behind him. Several had guns and one carried a coiled rope.

"I was taking a nap," Gary said plaintively. "Mr. Kurlacher came by to get Mrs. Spoonaker and she said I should wait until he brought her back."

Mr. Walker shoved Gary backward and Spike bared his teeth. Billy's father glared around the room. "Why should Kurlacher come get her?"

Gary shrugged. "I think it's because the honey he's selling is poisoned. That's what's making people sick."

"Let's search the house!" one of the men growled. "She's probably hiding."

The babble grew louder as the men spread out and went to each room in the cottage.

"I'm going to look in the shed and barn," Billy's father said. "That old woman never goes anywhere anymore. Some of you come with me."

Gary yawned again as he sauntered to the table with Spike at his heels. He picked up a piece of cookie and broke it to give half to his dog. The other half he stuffed into his mouth as he retreated to the living room sofa and sprawled out on it.

"You're a real smart kid, aren't you?" one of the

men said with a sneer. "If she really is gone, when will she be back, huh?"

"She said she'd be back before dark," Gary said, "but if she isn't, I'll have to leave. My mother doesn't like me to be out very late."

"Why didn't you let us in when we first knocked?" another man asked. "We nearly broke the door down!"

"I was sleeping," Gary said. "It takes me awhile to wake up when I'm really sound asleep."

"What was all that about Kurlacher's honey being poisoned? Where'd you get a story like that?" the first man asked.

"When Mrs. Spoonaker opened a jar of honey she could smell there was something wrong," Gary answered. "It's the chemistry in her body," he added.

"That's a lot of hogwash! She's a witch, that's what she is!"

Gary said nothing. It was no use arguing with a bunch of guys intent on mischief and angry besides.

Billy's father and his followers returned to the house, disgruntled and even more angry because they couldn't find the old woman.

"We might as well leave," Mr. Walker said. "If Kurlacher's with the old hag, he might not have the same idea about what to do with her that we have." He focused on Gary and his eyebrows came together as he glared. "You better keep your mouth shut, kid, if you know what's good for you," he said. "We don't need any sheriff to take care of this!"

Spike wrinkled his nose as he growled at the man. Gary nodded and then looked down at the floor. He hadn't realized he could lie so well, but a lie to protect a helpless old woman wasn't so bad, was it?

The men left, still arguing among themselves about Mrs. Spoonaker, although that isn't what they called her. Gary stayed on the couch until they had gone and he heard cars leaving. Then he rose and again locked the front door before he began to drag furniture off the rug and set chairs aside. The dishes rattled as he dragged the table, but he figured he had better hurry and get Mrs. Spoonaker out of the damp old cellar.

When he finally opened the trapdoor he stared down into darkness. "Mrs. Spoonaker?" he called. "They're gone."

A groan answered him and then her voice came eerily from the inky dark. "I'm afraid I can't get up, Gary. Can you come down and help?"

While Spike whined anxiously at the top, Gary went down the steps slowly, afraid he would step on her, but she was sitting on the bottom step and he knelt beside her. "What's wrong, ma'am?"

"It's my hip," she answered, exasperation in her voice. "It has stiffened because of the dampness and I cannot get up. Can you pull me to my feet? Maybe then I can make it up the steps."

Gary put a hand under each of the old woman's arms and used all his strength to help her struggle to her feet. The job was finally accomplished and then Gary got behind her and gently shoved her up each step to the top. Mrs. Spoonaker hobbled to a chair and Gary sat at the opening as they both panted for breath.

"Drat those rascals!" Mrs. Spoonaker exploded. "This is just too much! I'm going to tell Sheriff Thompson and have him speak to those dumb animals. That is, after I catch my breath."

"Do you want me to call him?" Gary asked.

"You had better get on home, Gary. Your mother will worry if you are late."

"Are you sure you'll be all right?"

A smile crinkled her already-wrinkled face. "I'll be all right, thanks to you. You might have saved my life, although for the life of me I can't believe they would have actually hung me." She sighed, then added, "I'll call Dr. Haines again, this time to bring help when he comes here this evening. Once the women believe the honey is causing the sickness, perhaps they can beat the idea into the men's heads. Then things should settle down."

Gary nodded. He was glad she hadn't seen the faces on the mob of men or the rope they had brought along. He had better get home and tell his mother about all this. She would know what to do.

CHAPTER ELEVEN

THE FUNERAL

GARY CLIMBED UP on Jock and headed for home, keeping a wary eye out to see if any of the men had stayed behind. There was no sign of them. Spike seemed to feel his master's unease for he, too, swiveled his head from side to side.

"Giddyup, Jock," Gary said, touching the pony's flanks. "We better make tracks for home, pardner." He grinned at the words. He couldn't have fought those men and won, but he sure fooled them. If he were a grown cowboy he would most likely have six-guns slung around his hips and then he could tackle even grown-ups. He sighed. Sometimes being just a kid was sure a nuisance.

When he arrived home, he unsaddled Jock and turned him into the pasture before going inside. Now he had to tell his mother what had happened. He knew he should have told her where he was going and now he wished he had. It just didn't seem to pay when you lied or kept things from your mother.

Mary was sitting in the living room watching television when Gary walked in. She wrinkled her nose at the set. "We're getting a new aerial next Thursday, but meantime this channel is really awful." Then she took a closer look at him. "What's the matter, honey? Did Jock act up again?"

"No, Mom. It's just . . . well, I rode out to Spoonaker's today and some men came out to kill her."

"Wha-a-at?" Mary asked, aghast. "Who tried to kill her and why?"

Gary sat down beside her and started telling her of the day's events. When he came to the part about the honey having been poisoned by bees gathering nectar from certain plants, she shook her head in wonder.

"Aren't we lucky that we don't like honey?" she asked. "Those poor people, especially Jimmy Allen. Who would ever think that honey that tasted like honey could kill? It's very fortunate Mrs. Spoonaker knows about things like that. Now Dr. Haines can help the ones who are still ill. And keep others from getting ill," she added.

After Gary finished telling her how Billy's father and the other men had come with a rope and guns and how he had helped the old woman hide in a cellar that nobody knew was there, his mother put her arm around him.

"Honey, I'm proud of you," she said, brushing a kiss across his forehead. "You must never lie to me, but fooling those terrible men was a good thing to do. Now we must make sure Mrs. Spoonaker isn't bothered again. I am going to phone Sheriff Thompson."

"Mrs. Spoonaker said she was going to call him, Mom."

"Well, I'll phone Mr. Kurlacher first and then the sheriff to make sure she talked to him."

When Mary told Mr. Kurlacher about the honey, he was aghast. "Now I wish I had tasted the stuff before I sold it," he said. "Only thing is, I can't stand the stuff anymore. I ate so much of it when I first had bees, it sort of turns my stomach now."

"We don't like it, either," Mary said. "Will you phone everyone you can and tell them not to eat any more?"

"I'll be glad to," Mr. Kurlacher answered, "only I doubt I will find many at home. Around here Sunday is visiting day and most will be out somewhere, especially with the weather so nice."

"Well, try later tonight or first thing in the morning," Mary urged. "I'll phone Dr. Haines now and he can help get the word around."

When Mary dialed the number for the doctor, the phone only rang and rang. The same thing happened when she tried to phone the sheriff. She cradled the receiver and frowned.

"A lot of people will be at the funeral tomorrow, Gary," she said slowly. "Dr. Haines will surely be there and so will Sheriff Thompson."

"What about Mrs. Spoonaker, Mom? Do you think she'll be okay tonight? If you couldn't get the sheriff, neither could she."

Mary dialed, then heard Mrs. Spoonaker say, "Hello."

"This is Mary Benson, Mrs. Spoonaker. May I come

get you so you can spend the night with us? I can't get the sheriff on the phone."

"Well, thank you, my dear, but that won't be necessary. I couldn't reach the sheriff either, but Fu has come to visit and that means he will be around for most of the night," the old woman said. Then she cackled and added, "Ask Gary how effective he is as a guard."

"Are you sure?" Mary asked doubtfully. "Gary said the men came to look for you with guns and a rope."

"I'll turn them into toads if they come again," Mrs. Spoonaker said. "That old cellar is too damp and dark to spend much time there."

Gary's mother frowned for a moment, then asked, "Well, may I pick you up in the morning? We're going to Jimmy's funeral and we would be glad to have you with us."

"Thank you, but no," she answered. "I hate funerals. Besides, the sight of me might rub salt into old wounds. I have never been able to convince them I'm not a witch, you see. Dr. Haines is coming by to pick up a tonic I've prepared and he can explain the illness to everyone."

Mary sighed. "Well, good night then. Phone me if you need anything."

Mrs. Spoonaker thanked her and hung up. Mary turned to answer the questions in her son's eyes. "She seems to feel safe where she is, honey. Apparently her owl is on duty tonight. She said if the men return she will turn them into toads."

Gary's eyes widened. "Can she really do that, Mom?"

Mary's eyes twinkled as she answered. "Anybody who can fly a broom around surely can do other magical things, don't you think?"

"Aw, you're making fun of me again, Mom."

"Let's fix some supper and then I will give you another lesson in chess, my most imaginative son," she said, her eyes still showing amusement.

Clouds rolled over Bellarosa during the night and were still keeping the surroundings gloomy as Gary and his mother prepared to go to Jimmy Allen's funeral. Word had gotten to them that school was closed for the day, as were most businesses in town.

"Do I have to look into the coffin, Mom?" Gary asked.

She eyed him for a moment before answering. "No, you don't, honey. The face of death is something that is hard to forget and I know you would rather remember your friend as he was when alive."

Gary breathed a sigh of relief.

"Have you been able to remember your father as he was while still alive? I shouldn't have allowed you to see him dead, but I was so grief-stricken at the time, I just didn't think."

Gary stared at her. How had she known he was having trouble seeing his father's real face because the one he had seen in the coffin kept coming between? But he couldn't stand seeing her feeling bad so he said, "Oh, sure, Mom. Remember the day we all went fishing and caught all those fish? Spike kept falling into the water because he was too little to know better and we had to keep fishing him out. Dad really laughed at him that day, didn't he?"

His mother smiled. "We all laughed a lot in those days," she said softly. Then she straightened. "Well, let's go."

The church was abuzz with whispering when they entered, but the preacher came from his office at the same time and everyone quieted. Jimmy Allen's mother sat in a front pew. She was clad all in black with a veil covering her face, and when the preacher began the eulogy, she sobbed into a black handkerchief.

Gary squirmed uncomfortably as he tried to think of anything but Jimmy lying dead. Had Dr. Haines spread the word that the honey was to blame and not Mrs. Spoonaker? Once they learned what had caused Jimmy's death, would they let the old woman alone? They should thank her, he thought indignantly. She had made a tonic with her herbs that would help cure honey poisoning.

When the eulogy had ended, the preacher led the way to the cemetery behind the church. Six pallbearers carried the small coffin between them as they trailed the preacher. Behind them walked Mrs. Allen, on the arm of Billy's father. The rest of the congregation came at the end of the procession and formed a circle around the hole that had been dug in the cemetery. The final blessings for Jimmy Allen were delivered and then his coffin was lowered into the ground.

Jimmy's mother sobbed into her handkerchief, then raised her head and wailed with anger. "I want my son avenged!" she said. "I want the witch who killed him dead!" She looked wildly around the assemblage. "Why have you people let this old woman terrorize you for so long? Why didn't you kill her long ago? Then my Jimmy would still be alive!"

There was a stunned silence, then Gary stepped forward. "Mrs. Spoonaker found what caused all the sickness—haven't you heard? Mr. Kurlacher's bees got into some poisonous plants and the honey did it."

"That's what you tried to tell us before," Billy's father said. "You're just a dumb kid, so what do you know?"

"He's right," Dr. Haines said. "I've distributed the tonic Mrs. Spoonaker prepared and my patients are recovering nicely."

"Folks, I'm sorry my bees caused all this trouble," Mr. Kurlacher said. "Hereafter I will taste each batch before I bring it to the store."

"That's hogwash!" Billy's father shouted. "That old hag should have been removed long ago."

Sheriff Thompson went to take him by the arm. "You are wrong, Walker. You incited a bunch of men to do harm to an old woman who is a credit to this community. If she wants to prefer charges, you will probably go to prison."

The congregation buzzed as people voiced their opinions about Mrs. Spoonaker and debated whether or not she was a witch. Billy Walker punched Gary on the arm, but Gary's mother kept a firm hold on her son so there would be no fighting.

"Mr. Walker, my son was a witness to the disgraceful events of yesterday," she said. "He will bear witness if Mrs. Spoonaker wishes to prosecute."

Several of the men who had been with Billy's father when they came after the old woman surrounded him, telling him again about the poisoned honey.

"Well, maybe the old woman wasn't at fault this time," Billy's father said, "but that old hag is a witch and should be put away."

"If I hear any more of that talk, Walker, *you'll* be put away!" Sheriff Thompson exclaimed.

"You leave my dad alone," Billy said threateningly. "He's right about the old woman being a witch, no matter it wasn't one of her spells that made everybody sick."

"If you will check, young Billy, you will discover that only people who ate the honey became ill," the sheriff said patiently.

"Yeah, and Mrs. Spoonaker fixed a tonic with the herbs she grows that eased it away," Gary said defiantly.

"Whadda you know?" Billy sneered.

"I know more than you," Gary answered. He faced the congregation. "If Mrs. Spoonaker *is* a witch, she's a *good* witch! Anyway, she's so far over the hill she needs our help sometimes and we better help her."

There were cries of agreement and a few grumbles of disbelief. Gary sighed. Once people got an idea in their heads it was sure hard to change them!

"Let's go home, Gary," his mother said.

"Could we go see Mrs. Spoonaker first, Mom?" he asked. "She might like to know how Dr. Haines and the sheriff and some of the others are standing up for her."

"Of course we can," Mary answered, then paused as a thought came to mind. "There has to be a way we can convince people she is a good woman. What if they saw it in print?"

"You mean like putting an ad in the newspaper?"

"Sort of, honey. Let's stop by home so I can call the *Journal*. If I can get a reporter to come interview Mrs. Spoonaker because she's the heroine who discovered the cure for the plague that was infesting the town, everyone can read about it."

"Let's get him to take her picture," Gary said. "She looks real nice and then even dummies who can't read will know she's famous."

When they reached home Mary called the newspaper office and asked for the editor. After talking to him for a short time, she hung up.

"What did he say?" Gary asked.

"He is sending a reporter to meet us at Mrs. Spoonaker's in an hour."

"We'd better get going, Mom. Mrs. Spoonaker will want to get ready to have her picture taken, won't she?"

"Oh, you know a lot about women, do you?" Mary teased. Then she nodded. "But you're right. Let's go."

Spike had greeted them joyfully and now he whined as he saw them preparing to leave.

"You better stay here, Spike," Gary said. "There's no use your tangling with that cat again. Mrs. Spoonaker might want him all smooth and calm to have his picture taken with her. Sit, boy!"

Spike sat down, then laid his head on his paws and gazed up at them with a look of mourning.

"He'll be all right, Gary," his mother said. "He can guard the house while we're gone."

"On guard, boy!" Gary said as they closed the door behind them.

When they reached their destination Mrs. Spoonaker

opened the door to greet them, then invited them inside. "Would you care for some tea?" she asked.

"You have to get ready to have your picture taken," Gary said.

"What?" she asked with a puzzled look.

Mary explained what was about to happen.

"Oh, dear," Mrs. Spoonaker said as she gazed around the room. "I haven't dusted for several days."

"You get yourself ready," Mary said. "Gary and I will tidy up while you do."

"I can dust, Mom."

"Okay, you dust and I'll straighten pillows and pictures," Mary said.

Soon a car pulled up behind Mary's and two men got out. One carried a camera. Mary opened the door.

"We're from the *Journal*, ma'am," one of the men said. "I am Jed Duval and this is my photographer, Dick Percy. Are you Mrs. Spoonaker?"

"No," Mary said with a smile. "Come in, gentlemen, and I will introduce you to Mrs. Spoonaker."

They entered and Mary introduced them all around.

"I understand you're a heroine," Jed said. "We would like to take your picture after you tell us the details of the honey poisoning and how you discovered and cured it."

Mrs. Spoonaker snorted as she smoothed her lap. "That young lad over there is a hero, if that's what you're looking for. He saved my life or I couldn't have saved anybody. Come over here, Gary Benson. If they want pictures, I want you in them with me."

With a shy grin, Gary walked to where Mrs. Spoonaker had indicated and sat beside her.

"You start, Gary," Mrs. Spoonaker said. "Tell them

how people in the town became ill and blamed me. Tell them how you saved me from the idiots who wanted to hang me."

Jed looked startled. "Why would anyone want to kill *you*, Mrs. Spoonaker?"

"Shut up and listen," she answered tartly. "When Gary finishes his part, then I'll tell you how an herbalist works."

The reporter grinned. "Is it all right if I tape this interview, ma'am?" At her nod of agreement, he started his recorder and Gary began the tale.

When Gary stopped speaking, Mrs. Spoonaker took over and explained how her herbs had cured the poisoned-honey sickness. Both men looked impressed as they listened to the account of the entire episode. When it was over, Jed moved away to give his photographer room.

"Ready?" Dick asked as he aimed his camera at Mrs. Spoonaker and Gary. "Smile," he said gently.

Gary and Mrs. Spoonaker looked at each other and grinned.

"Would you like my broom and cat in the photo, too?" the old woman asked.

The photographer looked puzzled.

"Never mind," Mrs. Spoonaker said. "I was only teasing."

The puzzled look remained on Dick's face, but he returned to his work and took several flash photos of the pair.

"You were both pretty brave," Jed said. "Thank you very much for the interview. It will be printed in tomorrow's edition."

"Can I have a copy?" Gary asked. "I've never been in a newspaper before."

Jed grinned. "I will personally send you each a dozen copies. This story will sell a lot of newspapers and I appreciate your calling us."

Mrs. Spoonaker breathed a sigh of relief as the door closed behind the two men. "I am really tired," she said. "I cannot stand so much strain anymore."

"We'll leave so you can take a nap," Mary said.

"I'll be back Saturday to work," Gary added.

Mrs. Spoonaker shook her head. "You are paid up, Gary. Without your help I would probably be dead by now. However, if you will consider helping me when you can and for pay, I'll sure be glad to have you."

Gary smiled. "I'll see you Saturday, Mrs. Spoonaker."

On the way home Gary and his mother were silent for a time, then Gary asked, "Is that all right, Mom? I mean, should I let her pay me?"

"I'm sure she would feel better if you did," Mary answered. "She is a proud woman and wouldn't offer if she couldn't afford it."

"Then I can help you, Mom. You can have my pay."

His mother smiled at him. "We'll add it to your college fund."

Gary thought for a time, then said, "Isn't it funny how much you have to do to get people to believe the truth? Do you think seeing Mrs. Spoonaker and the story in the paper will change Mr. Walker's mind?"

Mary laughed. "I doubt it," she answered. "He is so stubborn it will take a long time to change him."

"Too long a time, Mom."

"You are right, honey," Mary said as she shook her head.

"Oh, Mom! Please... please don't call me 'honey' anymore, okay?"

Mary's eyes twinkled as she glanced at him. "Yes, my smart son. What shall I call you? Sweetheart?"

Gary groaned. "How about just Gary?"

Mary laughed out loud, then said, "Okay, just Gary."